Francis Saltus

The Witch of Endor

and other poems

Francis Saltus

The Witch of Endor
and other poems

ISBN/EAN: 9783337391324

Printed in Europe, USA, Canada, Australia, Japan

Cover: Foto ©Andreas Hilbeck / pixelio.de

More available books at **www.hansebooks.com**

THE WITCH OF EN-DOR

AND OTHER POEMS

BY

FRANCIS S. SALTUS.

BUFFALO
CHARLES WELLS MOULTON
1891

BIGELOW PRESS: BUFFALO, N. Y.

FROM THE SHADOW OF THE SHADE

THIS WORK

WITH LOVING GRATITUDE

IS MOST AFFECTIONATELY

INSCRIBED

TO

THEODORE SALTUS

IN RECOGNITION

OF HIS LOVE AND KINDNESS

TO ME IN LIFE

AND TO MY MEMORY IN DEATH.

Friend, I am now beyond the Earth's affliction,
I speak unto thee from a Heavenly strand,
While Christ our Saviour gives me benediction,
And smiling, HOLDS MY HAND.

—FROM THE POEM OF JUDAS.

CONTENTS.

CONTENTS.

And I, who could have given him delectation,
  I, who with loves insensate ever burned,
  Was by my drowsy, dreamy monarch spurned,
But worshiped still in patient expectation.

*   *   *   *   *   *

Then the day came when Midianitish legions
  Assembled where the Shunem hills commence,
  And pitched thereon their desecrating tents,
And roamed and reveled through Gilboan regions.

And Saul, aroused from lethargy and sadness,
  Grew strangely troubled and was sore afraid ;
  His god of promises refused him aid,
And in his eyes there gleamed the fires of madness.

Distrust and fitful omens overfilled him ;
  Blinded with doubt he could not see his way ;
  Too proud to die, too vacillant to pray,
Visions of death and of disaster chilled him.

Then I, the scorned, the baffled, the unheeded,
  I, the poor outcast courtesan, the one
  He would not pitifully look upon,
I, the frail harlot who had vainly pleaded,

Bribed with my gold and ill-begotten treasure
  His falsest friends and made their households rich,
  And he was bidden by them to seek a witch,
Consult the stars and brave his God's displeasure.

And he gave heed unto them, broken-hearted,
  Weary of shallow nights and morbid days ;
  And through Manasseh, in quick, silent ways,
Unto En-dor I secretly departed.

There did I find, in wildernesses dismal,
  A cave forsaken amid all solitude,
  High in cold mountains where the eagles brood,
Above a precipice of depth abysmal,

Humid and dark, where noisome larvæ shimmered,
  Foul with dank reptiles and the stench of eft,
  By dizzy lightning at the summit cleft,   [mered.
And where the unwholesome moonbeams vaguely glim-

Now Saul had cast forth, by deluded fancy,
  Each ill-reputed wizard from the land ;
  And torments terrible had long been planned
For all who dealt in charms and necromancy.

And for a space I deemed some foulest hater,
    One I had bribed and pitilessly spurned
    When for my kisses amorous he yearned,
Had broken all trust and turned on me a traitor.

But no ! I heard his step, and doubt was shaken ;
    By night he came, and timorous, in disguise,
    In great extremity, with wandering eyes,
Fasting and pale, and by his God forsaken !

I met him at the cave's bleak door, convulsive,
    Wrinkled, in fetid rags, made foul by art,
    And lulled the soft throbs of my leaping heart,
Crouching before him, squalid and repulsive.

But under all this filthy abomination,
    Swathed in soft satin to my trembling knees,
    My redolent body burned in tempting ease,
Perfumed and gemmed I stood in expectation.

And though my lust restrained and new ambition
    Urged me to rush to him with arms outspread,
    With cunning shrewd I simulated dread
And in shrill tones asked then his wish and mission.

THE WITCH OF EN-DOR.

He told me all in stammering consternation,
   His vast desires, the longings of his soul,
   And, in dire anguish beyond all control,
Implored the succor of my incantation.

And I, the artful pythoness, to alarm him
   With subtle sorceries and hold him fast,
   Did fill with miasmal herbs a cauldron vast,
While muttering foolish syllables to charm him.

And at his feet, by cautious care assembled,
   I burned mephitic drugs and venoms dire,
   With adder skins and pestilential briar,
While he, my Saul, the strong one, watched and trembled.

Then by swift, dextrous tricks and transpositions,
   Before his credulous eyes I made pass by
   Majestic shapes, like those of gods on high,
Grim, hollow ghosts and woeful apparitions !

My tutored slaves, obedient as I willed it,
   Arose in glamoured mist and told to him
   All I had taught them in my earliest whim,
And awed his dumb, attentive heart and chilled it.

And by my rapid signs admonitory,
  Rising from doleful and phantasmal gloom,
  Before him suddenly did largely loom
The angered prophet Samuel, grave and hoary.

And as Saul gazed, bewildered and pathetic,
  With cold lips moving in unconscious prayer,
  Of all my wiles perfidious unaware,
The spirit spake in sentences prophetic.

And he who heard these ominous tones, affrighted,
  Fell prone unto the earth in livid fear,
  While I rejoiced to know and feel him near,
And pressed his nerveless form to mine, delighted.

*   *   *   *   *   *

Then, as he was a-hungered and most dreary,
  I bade my acolytes to swiftly bring
  A tender calf and slay it for the king,
To fortify the flesh unmanned and weary.

And in good haste with feverish palms I kneaded
  Flour, and did bake him there unleavened bread,
  While he, like some snake-tortured bird, in dread,
Gazed vacantly about and no thing heeded.

And yet with eagerness and hands unsteady,
  Of all my viands he partook with trust,
  And drained my wine that urged on eager lust,
The wine of dreamy herbs that I held ready.

And so, refreshed, he leaned upon my shoulder,
  And seeing no spectral harbinger of doom,
  Sought for his chanith in the murky gloom,
And finding it, grew confident and bolder.

Then to the hurrying winds that blew around us,
  I hurled the infamy of my disguise!
  And wanton-like, with large enamored eyes,
I kissed him, as imperious rapture crowned us.

In love's most tempting and delicious fashion
  I stood to dissipate his painful dream,
  Peerless in promise and in joy supreme,
Warm with my longing, with my hope, my passion!

And ere from dazzled torpor he could waken,
  Unto my breast I held my god, my all,
  My paradise, my ravishment, my Saul,
By fiercest ardor overcome and shaken!

Ah, God ! what ecstasy to hold him gladly,
   Chill to my lips, and dull his surly doubt
   With frenzied grasps and kisses, while without
The moaning winds thro' En-dor wandered madly !

Alone, alone with Saul ! Jehovah's chosen,
   The dominant king, the hero who had scorned
   My beauty irresistibly adorned,
No longer dumb, no longer mute and frozen,

But lover-like and by love's pangs demented,
   The amorous monarch of my dreams, who heard
   The story of my subterfuge, each word
And long caress that tempered it, contented !

And when I stammered forth in sighs and fever
   How I had made him mine, and blessed the guile,
   Heaven would revere the sweetness of his smile
And his fond pardon unto me, deceiver !

And, although struggling still with doubts pernicious,
   And all the wordless fears that loathe to die,
   Fresh confidence grew in him then, for I
Had tossed to gloom all broodings superstitious.

"Why did I know thee not," he cried, " of mortals
The perfect flower and fragrance?   I am strong,
And Saul thy king, and yet I did thee wrong,
Thou who hast turned me from death's very portals.

" For I, to-morrow, if the Lord doth spare us,
Will go with Jonathan my son and friend,
And strong Abinadab my son, to rend
The mongrel hordes that clamorously dare us.

"So tell me, queen of lissom sorceresses,
Dost thou not still betray thy trusting Saul?
Oh, answer fearlessly, didst thou see *all*
The wavering phantoms in their somber dresses?

"Didst thou behold or bring about the horrid
Dire shadow draped in mysteries of white,
The accusing figure of a Midianite,
That hurled dull blood unto my burning forehead?

"Dost thou, oh peerless Shumma mine, remember
Elusive shapes that answered not thy call,
Dim films of light abhorrent to thy Saul,
That rose *unquestioned* from thy cauldron's ember?

" Didst thou see *all?* " Yea, yea, again I told him.
   "This canst thou swear?"   Aye, have no foolish dread.
   And sighing, on his breast I drooped my head,
And with soft arms did languidly enfold him.

Gone were the visions terrible and hated,
   Gone were the pains my kisses strove to heal,
   While by his side, like a great ghost of steel,
His mighty, massive chanith scintillated !

*   *   *   *   *   *

And he went forth at day and left me sleeping,
   Alone within the dull cave's dawnless gloom,
   Unconscious of a sad, impendent doom,
Fond memories of his regal passion keeping.

And as I weary slept, he bent him over
   To cull the drowsy promise of my breath ;
   And then he went to Gilboa and to death,
Saul my beloved, my Benjamite, my lover !

To Gilboa perilous with armies teeming,
   Leaving me there, his slave, his love, his sin,
   To perish grandly in the battle's din,
While I in calm serenity lay dreaming !

FEAR.

The being supreme, that universes call
   God ; He who made us in His matchless might ;
   God, who exists in love, and song, and light,
Whose august name can doubting souls appall,

Disdains the humble homage of us all,
   Weak, puny motes His fiery glaive can smite,
   And scorns our prayers as age to age takes flight.
While the frail earth before Him bows, a thrall !

For he is tortured by intolerant dread !
   The dismal knowledge of *superior* powers
     That could annihilate him with a breath,
Thrills and dismays him, while, uncomforted,
   Among his myriad stars he trembling cowers,
     Filled with the unutterable fear of Death !

JEALOUSY.

Satan, an angel once in realms divine,
   The loved and chosen of God by his sweet grace,
   Dwelt with him in the miracles of space,
And worshiped with the hosts before his shrine.

But latent thoughts of perfidy malign,
   Dusked the strange glory of his perfect face,
   And God, who light in his dark soul could trace,
Hurled down to Hell the sinner saturnine !

Though stricken and ired, he did not then despair,
   Grimly remembering how he once implored
     And won, by haughty mien and accent proud,
The love of that vague creature, grandly fair,
   Whose awful beauty Heaven itself adored,
     And before whom God as a suppliant bowed !

EXTERMINATION.

A VISION.

With prescient sight that pierced the future's distance,
    Through countless centuries of doubts and fears,
I witnessed earth as it will have existence,
    In twice a million years !

On such grand lapses from time's pages sundered,
    I only dared to gaze in utter awe
Dazzled by new-born power, and while I wondered
    As in a dream, I saw

Vast, populous towns of contour Babylonian,
    Temples and palaces imperially rare,
Mazes of marble, grandiose and Neronian,
    Towering everywhere !

The teachings of the past seemed to engender
    Divinest art in methods most intense ;
All I beheld was beauty, form and splendor,
    Grace and magnificence !

All who breathed here, sons of forgotten races,
  Were of a new and lofty lineage proud ;
Moving in plastic strength, with regal faces,
  Haughty and Cæsar browed.

And I, whose eyes by God-like divination
  To all their secrets were no longer blind,
Read every thought that filled with exaltation
  The universal mind.

These creatures knew but one all-sacred duty,
  One cult to which the vilest would adhere,
A perfect love of pure impeccable beauty,
  Supreme, immense, sincere !

The poesy of broad skies, the moaning ocean,
  All Nature's glory, spoke not to their souls,
For art alone they held sublime devotion,
  Despising other goals.

No anthems filled the air, no psalms or psalters
  Praised the Creator who had given them birth ;
His name unknown was honored by no altar
  On this strange, perfect earth !

No voices sang harmonious Te Deums,
  No prayerful women bowed with pious plaints,
No roses sighed upon the mausoleums
  Of long-loved martyr saints !

The woe of Christ to them was but a story,
  A pleasing myth of legendary lore,
And in our God's unique, stupendous glory
  These men believed no more !

Then, as I gazed upon them in my dreaming,
  I saw a man with white, majestic head,
By frantic crowds, from every by-way streaming,
  Unto a grim cross led !

Spat on and stoned in his severe affliction,
  He calmly stood, nor did his glances quail ;
Helpless, I saw his odious crucifixion,
  Felt every rugged nail

That tore his feeble palms and feet asunder,
  And yet he shrank not in his pride august,
While the great hum of voices like a thunder
  Exclaimed, " His pain is just !"

And all the throng, the haughty and the lowly,
  Cried : " Peerless Beauty, may thy will be done !
This wretch upon our faultless earth all-holy
  Is now the only one !

" No shame, no torture can be too unlawful
  To free from his vile feet the ground he trod,
For he who writhes before us, pale and awful,
  Dared to believe in God ! "

1877.

MISREPRESENTATION.

In desolate dreams, whose memory terrific
 Will haunt me to my life's unhappy close,
The ghost of Christ, our Savior beatific,
 Disconsolately rose !

Sad years have flown, but still to me are vivid
 The angry fevers in His piercing eyes,
As He before me stood, erect and livid,
 But Godlike in no wise.

The bleeding palms and feet, the blond beard tangled,
 Were changed not since the dolorous day of death ;
I saw the thorn-pressed brow, the lean side mangled,
 And heard His hot, quick breath !

But marked with stupor that no sign of meekness
 Dwelt in that face, still marvelously fair,
And that His lips were curled in scornful weakness,
 While no prayer lingered there.

And He, whose pure, imperishable glory
  The fears of men for ages did assuage,
He, the unique, the sweet, the salvatory,
  Stood pallid in strong rage.

And with vindictive voice upon me calling,
  This poor Redeemer, bartered, murdered, sold,
To me, mute, shivering mortal, an appalling
  And hideous story told,

Which, were it known, and could mankind conceive it,
  This strange weird vision most sublimely sad,
Would fill with awe the minds that dared believe it,
  And make whole nations mad.

For in this tale of sacrifice and error,
  Monstrous narration of bewildering things,
I understood at last Christ's pain and terror,
  His unknown sufferings !

With words that scorched like fire my very being,
  As I before him palpitantly sighed,
He cried out loudly : " Man, thou now art seeing
  One that was crucified !

" I tell to thee, and verily, oh dreamer,
    By all the gory horror of my brow,
That I, God's Son, was loftier and supremer
    On earth than I am now !

" For I, like thee, once knew rare dreams Elysian,
    When, a pure child, dim centuries ago,
I first beheld in sleep a dazzling vision,
    And heard a voice say low :

" ' *Arise, thou chosen of the Lord ! and ponder*
    On these my dictates, upon these my words.
The breath of Heaven is in thee ; rise and wander
    Forth among beasts and birds.

" ' *Preach unto man my laws humane and holy,*
    For thou of earth are not, but most divine;
Preach on the gold of thrones, in hamlets lowly,
    The grandeur which is mine.

" ' *Be faithful, meek and chaste ; the power is given*
    To thee even now all souls to blindly sway ;
While God, omniscient in the heart of Heaven,
    Will guide thee on thy way.

"' *More than a king, gem-crowned, in Syrian raiment,*
  Greater than worshiped prophets wilt thou be,
For thou shalt never die, nor will base payment
  Be even taken of thee.

"' *Jehovah his proud equal now doth make thee,*
  Until thy glorious mission shall be done ;
And through life's gloom his light will ne'er forsake thee,
  Oh, blessed, anointed one ! '

" Then o'er me came divinest inspiration,
  Knowledge and wisdom grew within my mind,
And love, like some delicious revelation,
  Dawned for entire mankind.

" And I went forth feeling new joys immensely,
  For pride had flown to my unsullied heart,
And I revered this august God intensely,
  Of whom I seemed a part.

" How could I doubt, when sense of love and pardon
  Which my weak soul before had never felt,
With infinite pity that no scorn could harden,
  Sudden within me dwelt ?

"Therefore, immaculate, with resignation,
    Out to the traitorous world I humbly went,
Destined in holy ways for man's salvation,
    Meek and benevolent.

"Yet often, alas! dire thoughts would vex and grieve me :
    What if all were an idle dream or whim?
What if this subtle guardian did deceive me?
    Why place my trust in him?

"But heavenly voices, when these doubts came o'er me,
    Sang faith back to my soul and made it true,
While radiant hands of light would point before me
    The path I should pursue.

"So, confident, I trod the vales Judean,
    Loved by the sick, the famished and the lame,
While one incessant eulogistic pæan
    Hailed my redeeming name!

"By all revered, and fearing no detraction,
    Conscious of subtle and undying powers,
I blessed and saved with *human* satisfaction
    Among Samarian bowers.

" The sea and land in slavish ways obeyed me,
　My miracles spread hope through all the land,
For God himself was there to urge and aid me,
　And guide my healing hand.

" And yet I, cynosure of all, would wonder
　Why, if I were divine, should common greed
Creep through my veins, imperiously sunder
　And shake my rooted creed !

" Why should I feel, I, pure and vision-laden,
　A ravishment, a yearning, a surprise,
When in dusk hours some flower-like Hebrew maiden
　Gazed in my answering eyes ?

" I knew not until reason proved me tempted,
　Then from the warm allurement I would flee,
For God, I felt, from sin had not exempted
　The flesh, vile part of me !

" Ah now, while my poor spirit wanders sphereless,
　Alone in incommensurable space,
I still remember those delicious, peerless,
　Sweet dreamy days of grace,

"When throngs adoring, in that past existence,
  Kissed with quick, eager lips my passing hem,
While white before me in the sapphire distance
  Rose towered Jerusalem.

"Ah ! I recall with tomb-touched memories tender
  The Mount of Olives, and each fruitful tree
That nursed blithe birds above the gem-like splendor
  Of lakes like Galilee.

"By Him at that hour I was not forsaken,
  For in the inner essence of my soul,
Poesy's charm to me He did awaken,
  And gave me its control.

"Then I than earth's most noble bards was greater,
  And on my lips inspired there ever hung
The unuttered canticles of my creator,
  Songs that no man has sung.

"And I remember those departed glories,
  When Kedron's vales re-echoed linnets' songs,
And how I charmed with texts and allegories
  The vast, attentive throngs ;

" And when with my disciples, friends and leaders,
  I roamed where spring had made Gennesaret green,
And how amid fair Bethany's tall cedars
  I preached my creed serene ;

" With John beside me, Matthew, James and Peter,
  The upright Andrew, the confiding Jude ;
Men whose allegiance and whose love made sweeter
  The strange life I pursued.

" And I recall those nights when, charmed, I listened
  To music of soft ugabs and shophars,
While the blue depths of calm Tiberias glistened
  Beneath a world of stars.

" Alas ! the enchantment passed, while fast and faster
  Continuous evil fell upon my head ;
I, the world's benefactor, guide and pastor,
  Was into ambush led.

" Yet faith had utterly and blindly filled me,
  For I had healed with my caressing touch,
And men who, were I powerless, would have killed me,
  Worshiped and marveled much.

" From rabid bodies I had cast forth demons,
   And I amid the human hordes, elect,
Could purify the sins of lawless lemans,
   And dead men resurrect.

" No leprous churl, no wretch consumed of cancer,
   No weeping boor possessed of searching pain,
Spake unto me, to whom I did not answer:
   ' Go free of fear and stain! '

"And I, who hearkened to their prayers and praises,
   I, who had heard them call, upon my way,
' Hail to the King who flesh from darkness raises! '
   Did marvel more than they.

" Then came the time when I, the gentle master,
   Was sorely tempted by the wiles of Hell ;
Disgrace, derision and supreme disaster
   Upon my calm life fell.

"Scoffed at in insolent ways, but still undaunted,
   I reed-like bowed before my shame unique,
Although my every step was tried and taunted,
   Although I could not speak

"Or curse the fools that harmed me, for those voices,
　Those suave seraphic voices I had heard,
Murmured : '*Thy Father in thy strength rejoices !*
　Utter no hasty word !'

"And in the depths of my great degradation
　I found new fervor for the coming strife,
And, hopeful, felt in my humiliation
　That God would grant me life.

"So, when poor Judas, one whom I had trusted,
　One who had shared with me my bread and home,
One whose weak brain for paltry silver lusted,
　Sold me to pagan Rome,　.

"I pitied him, and pardoned him, and waited,
　Knowing I would receive celestial aid ;
And with strong faith intact and unabated
　Unto the Unknown prayed.

"But, shame ! oh shame ! my enemies and foemen
　Dragged me from sweet Gethsemane, and bound,
Before one Pontius Pilate, judge and Roman,
　I stood, and no word found !

"Certain that he would haughtily and proudly
 Cry : ' Nazarene, this is my just decree :
Get thee now forth, oh holy man ! for loudly
 My voice proclaims thee free !'

" But he, a timorous hireling, would not save me,
 And to the rabble clamoring at his side
He cried, ' I give Barrabas,' and he gave me
 There to be crucified !

" Then odious doubt o'erwhelmed me swift and horrid.
 Was I abandoned in this dire distress ?
The sweats of death oozed chill upon my forehead,
 I was all wretchedness.

" For how could he, this God superb and powerful,
 Take life like mine, when he had said to me :
' More great than Kings thou shalt be on the flowerful
 Green slopes of Galilee !'

" No, no ! my righteous hopes were not prostrated ;
 Surely, I thought, I can not perish here !
Enoch, Elijah were to Heaven translated,
 Why should I foster fear ?

"So, blind with doubt and hideous dread repulsive,
  I wept not when the crowds that wished my loss
Dragged me forth thorn-crowned, palpitant, convulsive,
  To that world-worshiped cross!

"And though the heavy, huge nails rent and tore me,
  Although mine eyes in agony grew dim,
I saw the martyr's promise shine before me,
  And still believed in Him!

"And there beside me in the gloom, repenting,
  A thief called loudly on my worthless name.
I pardoned him, for the last time relenting,
  Waited, but no help came.

"Oh man, oh man! I then called out in anguish:
  'God, why forsake me? Now recall Thy words!
"Oh Lama Lama Sabachthani, I languish!"
  Hear me!' But no one stirred!

"Ah! then I knew by lies he was degraded,
  And on my cheeks there rose the red of shame;
Disgust resistlessly my mind pervaded,
  Like a quick leaping flame!

" And from my lips, like some swift loosened torrent,
　A withering curse to Heaven, in my despair,
Unheard of man, rang out supreme, abhorrent,
　Upon the deathless air !

" I now can scorn all hatred to dissemble,
　But I say to thee, mortal that thou art,
Its utter anguish would have made God tremble,
　Had he possessed a heart !

" Gaze in my pallid face, my worn eyes tearful,
　Look at my lacerated palms that bleed,
Gaze on my body scourged, and thin, and fearful,
　Thou of my race and creed !

" And seeing me here, borne down by Fate's contention,
　Learn from my lips the awful truth, that when
I died, God gave me not the grand ascension
　Believed by many men.

" Cast out of Heaven and Hell, my woeful spirit
　Is no more great or less than *thine* will be ;
No realms of peace did my sad soul inherit,
　There is no rest for me !

" Betrayed, beguiled, an object of derision,
  For hours upon the cross I hung ! In song
Tell unto men, oh man, thy truthful vision,
  Sing of my nameless wrong !"

*   *   *   *   *   *

Then the sad silence of my vision rending,
  I heard a wail of terrible despair,
And saw a hundred spectral hands descending,
  Clutch at his gory hair . . . . . !

'Twas o'er !   The martyr ghost far from me fluttered.
  Sighing, I woke, and gaining thought's control,
Suddenly felt the truth of all he uttered !
  And terror seized my soul ! . .

ULTIMA THULE.

My fancy shuns all fair historic land ;
  No white Alhambra, vested by orange trees,
  Or laughing Como, can my sorrow please ;
For me Greece is not fair, Rome is not grand.

Merry with birds and buds, each sunny strand
  That I behold can no regret appease,
  And I am mute before the glory of seas
That kiss green shores where marble temples stand.

I seek the landscape of my dreams, a spot
  Scorched barren by the lightning's lurid blight,
    Alike by timorous man and beast unsought,
Where stars, and sun, and hope, and God are not,
  And where the sad, unalterable night
    Is dark and desolate as my every thought.

1878.

ABRAHAM.

And Abraham, son of Terah, in distress,
Bent low his brows, and in all wretchedness
  Cried: " Lo! I, guardian of the Jewish nation,
    Have cruelly and rashly sent away
    The gentle offspring of my love this day
  Unto the bitter desert's desolation!

" I, who am rich in flocks and many herds,
Have greatly sinned, for, with unfeeling words,
  I Ishmael bade with Hagar, my handmaiden,
    To seek Beersheba's solitudes of sands,
    And leave the pleasure of my pasture lands,
  With little bread, with water lightly laden.

" Far to the danger of an arid tomb
I sent them mournfully, for Sarah's womb,
  Gladdened by Isaac, strangely born, was jealous.
    Ah, God! I hearkened to her and repent!
    Upon me visit not thy discontent;
  To save and free them now my soul is zealous.

"No peaceful calm my wrinkled brows will bless,
Until the red and sultry wilderness
    Restores to me the lives I have molested ;
        Remorseful, I am fain to kiss their feet,
        And bow before them in my woe complete ;
    For days my guilty conscience has not rested.

"Oh Ishmael, my sweet son ! I long to speak
My whole love to thee, injured and most meek
    Of all the seed the Lord Jehovah sent me !
        Thy form emaciate in phantasmal light
        Haunts me with starving lips at dawn, at night.
    Hear me, forgive me, son ! I do repent me !

"Like the wind's ravage in a field of flowers,
Oh Ishmael, my beloved, in hapless hours
    Heartless I did renounce the love I gave thee ;
        But now that thou art helpless and unclaimed,
        Now that my every fiber throbs ashamed,
    Ishmael, my child ! I will depart to save thee !"

And Abraham, by a deep remorse possessed,
Was fain to hasten in paternal quest
    Of Ishmael, and with diligence he bent him,

And much consoled by firm resolve and trust,
He bowed his weary brow unto the dust,
Praying for strength, and this Jehovah sent him.

And so, upon that day, it came to pass
He bade his servants load a nimble ass
With many meats and juicy figs delicious,
White leavened bread and hoards of golden wheat,
With healing herbs and gourds of water sweet,
Imploring of the Lord to be propitious.

And in his trembling age he left his tents,
Contrite and weeping for his grave offense,
By many prayers his many fears disarming,
And with him took unto Moriah's sod
Isaac, his son trained in the cult of God,
The child of prophecy, devout and charming,

Isaac, the love and promise of his eyes,
Isaac, his son, submissive, meekly wise,
To teach with kind solicitude and tender,
And show to him new countries, where Tamar's
Stupendous towers beneath the Orient stars
Shone in their haughty and embattled splendor.

And as they wandered through the desert wild
He told unto the shy, attentive child
  Strange legends of the past and wondrous stories
    Of Noah, the ark and the redeeming dove,
    Of Enoch's faith and of Jehovah's love,
  Of Adam's sin and of Edenic glories.

He spoke of the great flood that marred the world,
By God indignant to destruction hurled,
  When He in myriad waters grandly thundered ;
    He told of Cain's red, bitter crime, and how
    God set a mark upon his livid brow,
  While the delighted child in rapture wondered.

In such wise were the weary moments passed,
But in the torrid desert scorched and vast
  No sign of Hagar came upon the morrow,
    And in the pitiless and blinding sand,
    Chartless, irresolute and most unmanned,
  The humbled patriarch mourned in direst sorrow.

The path no more was clear unto his eyes
Beneath the intolerant glare of sullen skies.
  Aimless as wind-blown leaves he went and wandered,

With none to guide him on the ardent way,
The sand alone around him, and dismay
Seized his strong heart, while desolate he pondered.

"Fit punishment is this!" he cried, and fell
Where death dawned livid unto Ishmael.
  "God has ordained that I and mine shall perish!
    Here in this waste, parched, destitute and numb,
    I must await the vengeance that will come
To rob me of the only son I cherish!"

The agonizing thought all hope dismayed;
In vain, and knowing prayer in vain, he prayed,
  And of all sinning bitterly repented!
    The torrid twilight swooned upon his pain,
    And then upon the broad and boundless plain,
Clasped in his arms the suffering child lamented.

On acrid herbs and locusts then they fed,
In harrowing distress uncomforted,
  Until even these with arduous searching failed him,
    And Abram's mind, as one struck down by plague,
    Wandered in sad confusion vexed and vague,
While languors he had never known assailed him.

.Madness as sudden as a leaping flame
Burst on his hoary forehead marked by shame,
    And in a trance he heard a voice mysterious
        Cry : " Abram, expiate thy cruel crime !
        In thy distress be patient and sublime,
    Poor Hagar's voice cries out in wrath imperious.

" Sacrifice Isaac, glory of thine eyes !
The God who thy fidelity now tries,
    Though cruel, still retains sweet balm of pardon ;
        Give unto him thy only treasured son,
        Isaac, the one thou lovest to look upon ;
    Before his frailty let thy warm heart harden."

And Abram, harking to the voices, cried :
" Oh God ! thou didst unto me say in pride,
    When in thy graciousness my soul did slumber,
        That like the perfect stars that haunt the sky,
        And like the sand-grains that about me lie,
    My seed would be in beauty and in number !

" Yet now in anguish must I slay my son,
The one I pitifully look upon,
    The guardian of my future and my token !

If I should take his guiltless life away,
As Thou ordainest on this hateful day,
Will not Thy promise, God august, be broken ?"

But stronger voices cried again : " Obey !
Obey ! Prove now thy rooted trust and slay !
  God's wrath by thy enormous tribulation
    Must be appeased, and by the awful deed ;
    Although thy father-heart must swell and bleed,
The sacrifice will gain thee sweet salvation ! "

And Abram said to Isaac : " Now behold !
By visions terrible and manifold,
  Jehovah warns me that this hand has doomed thee ;
    Thou must submit to Heaven's divine decrees,
    With joy and prayer, and on thy bended knees,
For all the tempests of His ire have gloomed thee ! "

Then Isaac lifted up his weary head,
And in a murmur, like a faint wind, said :
  " Weep not, my father, by the Great One chidden !
    Beyond the anguish here my eyes see light !
    Obey, before I die of thirst, and smite !
Do thou as God has mercifully bidden."

But Abram, hunger-mad, heard not his words ;
Around them hovered gaunt, ill-omened birds,
 Eager as he for flesh and sweet nutrition.
  Then on his son's pale, shriveled limbs he gazed,
  And like a beast by fiercest famine crazed,
 He craved his blood in brutal inanition.

A mist of red arose before his eyes,
And with a cry that would God agonize,
 Hot hunger in his heart of desolation,
  He stood erect amid the sands that hour,
  With hideous glances, eager to devour
 His child, his blood, his Isaac, his salvation !

And as the guilty patriarch raised the knife
To immolate that pure and sacred life,
 The lips of Isaac opened and, enraptured,
  He cried : " Oh father, see ! " and, fear-compelled,
  He turned and saw a struggling ram withheld
 By firm resisting brambles bound and captured.

Then, ravenous, he rushed upon the prey,
And cruelly and swiftly he did slay
 The brute appalled, draining his life-blood madly,

And, when the flesh his craving did appease,
Bloody and trembling, on his aged knees
He fell and praised the Lord Jehovah gladly.

Then Isaac moaned forth weakly : " Father, dear,
Hath mercy touched the heart of God austere ?
Hath He, omnipotent, seen well to save me,
Or hath He done so for dear Ishmael's sake ? "
And Abram turned his head and said : " Partake
This food in ways miraculous He gave me."

*   *   *   *   *   *

And Abram turned unto his home and sod,
And to the people there he told how God
Had tried his faith, and how he had not blundered.
But Isaac marveled and, with downcast eyes,
Gazed on his father with a strange surprise,
But spake no word, while all the people wondered.

1880.

MOOD OF SORROW.

I strolled into the green heart of a wood,
One sunny summer noon, in quest of shade,
But all to me seemed somber and dismayed.
The trees were wan, buds bloomed not as they should;

Nature serene ne'er bore a darklier mood.
I heard no sound; bright butterflies arrayed
In gorgeous tints lurked in the reeds afraid;
I found a dead bird there, and understood.

For its sweet sake flowers droop and calm winds grieve;
Crickets its funeral song will sadly drone ;
And leaves will fall its tender breast to shield.
Some friendly spider will its silk shroud weave,
And, oh my God! I, friendless and alone,
See grim before me loom the potter's field.

ACCUSATION.

SCENE.—A roadside in Galilee; Christ with His Disciples passes. A devil addresses him, after having been cast forth from a man possessed.

"So thou hast cast me forth and art elated
To see me here, undone, humiliated,
   And by thy saintly majesty oppressed ;
I, of great Satan's acolytes the boldest,
While now command thou arrogantly holdest
   Over the useless flesh that I possessed,

"Yon odious beggar, haggard and mephitic,
With face impure and gaunt limbs paralytic,
   Fetid with vermin, foul with all disease,
Who now stands clamoring by thy mantle loudly,
Hailing in boorish veneration proudly
   Thy deeds miraculous and thy prodigies !

"Thy simple word from his base form expelled me,
Thy hand august in holy horror held me,
   And as a wind that carries chaff away,

Thy prayers have swept me from his bones tormented,
While I, rebellious and most discontented,
    Am forced thy rigorous mandates to obey !

"But no sweet sign of thine can ever urge him
To paths of righteousness again, and purge him
    From my time-clinging and disastrous stain,
For he is doomed in primal sin to linger,
And the soft touch of thy consoling finger
    To heal his tainted soul has been in vain !

"I was cast forth, I, Devil, who hate malignly,
Before thine anger as it warmed divinely,
    But my disgrace is tempered in its smart;
For I say to thee, marvelous restorer,
No grace of thine can cleanse thy vile adorer,
    Or purify the hell that holds his heart.

"The utter truth of these my words thou knowest,
For on thy brow impassible thou showest
    To me, even now, a sad, reluctant dread !
Oh Jesus ! wise and holy man, elected
By His decree and by a God protected,
    How by my arts wast thou in error led !

" Affecting once to spurn and to despise me,
With mien all insolent thou didst exorcise me
    Before the rabble of the road and town.
But tell me, prophet, didst thou not dissemble?
If not, why dost thou blanchen now and tremble,
    Conscious of crime, with humble eyes cast down?

" I scorn thy sanctity, supreme and natal,
For thou well knowest thy odious fault and fatal;
    Lured by my wiles a God thou hast betrayed!
Better for thee hadst thou allowed me, quiet,
Within the carrion of my choice to riot,
    Than thy sublimity to have displayed.

" For I tell to thee, visionary, dreamer,
False seer, false prophet, insincere redeemer,
    Doomed to my hate and to immortal fame,
That thou, like some frail reed by tempests stricken,
Wilt cower aghast while all thy blood will quicken,
    When thou hast heard the meaning of my name.

" I was cast forth by thee, elate, insulting,
But, unabashed, in my defeat exulting,
    I now unto thy borrowed power reply,

That I, than thou, of future calm am surer,
That I, though soiled and sad, than thou am' purer
 That I immortal am, while thou shalt die!

" To do my task allotted I have striven;
To thee another grander one was given,
 And heaven was thine if thou didst not betray ;
Now thou hast sinned, while terrible and tearful
Thy life will be in coming trials fearful,
 And this with joy I tell to thee to-day!

" Ah ! the white pallors of thy forehead darken !
Christ, ere I go, unto my last words hearken,
 And vex me with anathemas no more.
Answer, mock Savior, why didst thou eject me
From that low begging clod, and not detect me
 In other guise and cast me out before ?

" How, with thy gifts of divination glorious,
Didst thou not find and hurl me forth victorious
 From far more tainted flesh than his, the time
When thou, oh God ! *aware* of my temptation,
Didst fail to scorn hell's subtle intimation,
 And fearlessly descended into crime ?

"Thou shrinkest ! It was *I* who, mute and wary,
Possessed before the form impure of Mary,
  One who is called and is the Magdalene,
One who had cloyed thee with her fond caresses,
Who bathed thy feet with unguents and soft tresses,
  One on whose breast thy forehead thou didst screen!

" Ah ! thou art contrite now and strangely livid !
The sin I hail upon thy cheeks is vivid !
  Shaken and dumb, thou hast no right to doubt !
In that vague hour, oh ! guilty mighty Master,
In that strange hour of peril and disaster,
  Why in thy strength didst thou not cast me out ?

"What charm had she to change thy sacred mission,
Sow in thy veins the seeds of all perdition ?
  How could her will so suddenly enmesh
Thy holiness and purity forever,
And all thy future happiness dissever
  By her unholy and polluted flesh ?

" Ah ! canst thou think that I, grown feeble-hearted,
From her low loins at thy first touch departed,
  That I was slavish to thy will ? Oh, no !

Thy tones were faltering and thy passions wandered ;
Too long upon her grace thy spirit pondered ;
  Thy voice abjuring me was faint and low.

" Unnerved and dazzled by her lissome beauty,
Didst thou with upright heart fulfill thy duty ?
  Was thy bland soul weighed down by thoughts
    devout ?
Ah, Christ ! I tell thee in fierce jubilation,
Hell dragged thee there from thy grand elevation !
  Why, doubly warned, didst thou not cast me out ?

" Thou answerest not ! Where is thy vaunted valor ?
Thy brow is hueless in ignoble pallor.
  Man of great marvels, thou art strangely dumb.
Thy sin upon thee as spilt blood is scarlet,
For thou before the allurement of a harlot
  In sacrilegious passion didst succumb !

*   *   *   *   *   *

" Enough ! Thy grouped and worn Disciples yonder
Wonder at thy delay and gravely ponder ;
  Go, go thy destined way and meet thy fates !

Heal, soothe and pray, sad object of my pity,
And turn thy steps unto the towerful city,
　　Where in the dreamy dusk thy Mary waits.

" Go to thy cross, and as thou goest, teaching
Consoling creeds, when thou thy faith art preaching,
　　Remember, in the moaning of the wind
My voice will haunt thee and hell's mocking laughter,
Exultant in its scorn, will follow after
　　One who has grievously and greatly sinned !"

Feb. 1, 1879.

SONNET.

I can not love the myriad flakes of snow
  That fall so gently over mead and moor ;
  To my spleen-fostered mind they are too pure ;
Their white, chaste secrets I can never know.

Dark tides of discontent within me flow ;
  Such rare perfection I can not endure.
  That which delighteth the untutored boor
Leaves me despondent, and I fain would go

To some far tropic land where insolent flowers,
  Gorgeously colorful, bloom but a day,
    Where deadly perfumes scent the torrid air,
And where, like my strange thoughts, in snaky bowers
  I could see Nature in superb decay
    Be beautifully rank and foully fair.

Feb. 23, 1878.

CAIN.

I roamed the young, fair earth for happy hours,
  When the first dawns upon its grace ascended,
  Seeking its virgin secrets unattended,
Hailing the new-born flowers.

I was a tiller of the blooming ground,
  The proud possessor of broad meadows vernal,
  And in the doing of my task diurnal
My happiness was found.

I loved my liberal land where cattle teemed,
  My sunny slopes, my fair and fecund valleys,
  And through the rustle of my leafy alleys
I wandered and I dreamed.

My soul was warmed with song. I worked elate,
  Glad of my noble toil and nothing fearing,
  My God august religiously revering,
Conscious that He was great.

Nature was fresh as I in those new days,
   And though my sire from Eden had been ejected,
   I knew his sin, and God's decree respected,
And, knowing it, gave Him praise.

Life unto me was utter joy ; the light
   And splendor of my vast Creator filled me ;
   The magnitude of His omniscience thrilled me ;
He was my day, my night.

Screened by His guarding hand, I lived secure,
   I, the first flesh, born at the world's beginning,
   For He had harmed me not for Adam's sinning,
But, pardoning, left me pure.

Abel, my brother, perfect and most blessed,
   The chosen of my soul, was ever near me ;
   His fond, fraternal merriment would cheer me
When I was sore oppressed.

And wealth was mine in plenty, and I had
   Wives, blonde as swaying wheat, content and duteous,
   Caressing sisters, children fair and beauteous,
And all these made life glad.

And, when I left fatigued the furrowed sod
  To seek my home and gain their joyous greeting,
  My happiness by all their own completing,
I knelt and worshiped God.

*   *   *   *   *   *

But ah! their gentleness could not appease
  His thirst for servile prayer, and He did shun them,
  And on a day of wrath did cast upon them
A scourge and a disease.

I could not quell it, as they lay there stark,
  But, high above this scene of lamentation,
  I felt God reveled in my desolation,
And all my soul grew dark.

Doubt dawned, for He, the omnipotent, the strong,
  No longer lent the beauty of His blessing
  To those who loved Him, and in foul transgressing,
I brooded on my wrong.

My wrong; for He whom I had much besought,
  He who had in His holy image made me,
  Had wrecked my many prayers and had betrayed me.
The thought burned as I thought!

Forth in the glades where I had slept and sighed,
   With harrowing hesitations then I wandered,
   And deep in soundless solitudes I pondered
On His preposterous pride !

I saw life blooming insolent and rare
   Around me with a keener, subtler wonder ;
   I saw life rule the earth above and under ;
I saw life everywhere.

Nature alert, perpetually new,
   Rose green before me, by that Maker's choosing,
   And as I watched it in my somber musing,
A thought stupendous grew !

"Oh God!" I cried ; "whom once I could adore,
   I, then so humble, *now* a loyal hater,
   Will mar thy work, most insolent creator,
Now and forevermore !

"My brawny arms will proudly sweep away
   Before thine eyes each thing on earth now living,
   And to destroy thy work, I, unforgiving,
Prepare in wrath to-day !

"Thy majesty my soul can not appall !
The tender earth is young and unencumbered;
All creatures having life are known and numbered,
And I, Cain, know them all!

"These will I slay, my wives and servants dear,
My laughing children, and my welcome brother,
My venerated sire, my white-browed mother,
All, and without a tear!

"I will not heed the tempting of a sigh,
To no compassionate call will I be pliant;
All, all shall die before Thee! Then, defiant,
Before Thee I shall die!

"Yea! thou shalt look upon a desert bare,
And clamor in vain for praise and anthems loudly,
While I alone will live to answer proudly,
' *Thou shalt have no more prayer!* '

"Then, with my angry insults to the sky,
Unflinchingly my presence will pursue Thee,
And, when I choose to cease to speak unto Thee,
Then, only, will I die!"

  * * * * * *

I paused and listened with hot, hurried breath,
  Erect, accepting all, alone, firm-hearted,
  And hearing then no answering voice, departed
To give life unto death !

So, for unnumbered days, in wrath I slew
  Alike the harmless birds, the beasts ferocious,
  Without a pang or pain, in calm atrocious,
As I had sworn to do.

The swarming rivers, winding to far seas,
  By offal foul and carrion I polluted,
  And, by the mastery of my hate imbruted,
I felled the blooming trees.

Far to the winds I flung the unrooted seed,
  From out the soil I tore the young buds growing,
  I burned the bounteous orchards overflowing,
And I was glad indeed !

In every path my sateless rages toiled ;
  I moved attended by all desolation,
  And by the marvels of my desecration
I gloried as I spoiled.

No marah then was mine, and in my pride
  Successful, unabashed and most exulting,
  God at each step defiantly insulting,
I unto Abel cried :

" The Lord hath told me in a dream His whim ;
  Harken therefore unto His will, oh brother !
  Prepare a firstling from thy flock, none other,
And sacrifice to Him.

" While I, with offerings gathered from my trees,
  Most humble fruit of unpretending savor,
  Will strive to gain His providential favor,
And by my worship please."

And pious Abel, trusting in my love,
  Glad in such sacrifice to be partaker,
  Did burn a lamb as offering to his maker,
With all the fat thereof.

Even then, I say, in my contempt severe,
  Grandly, fraternally, I would have pardoned,
  And melted by my tears a spirit hardened,
Had I not known God near ;

God, who had seen the savory gift and sweet ;
   God, who was eager for our genuflection ;
   God, who delighted in our base subjection,
Our servitude complete !

I felt that He, invisible, was nigh ;
   His great mysterious essence hovered o'er me ;
   I felt his moody majesty before me,
And with a savage cry,

Powerful enough to awe His holihead,
   My hosts of hate against Him fast assembling,
   Cruel, sublime, magnificent, untrembling,
I struck my brother dead !

And as I staggered, with hot arms defiled,
   Warm with the blood of him I loved, yet tearless,
   Gazing upon the face of God and fearless,
I arrogantly smiled !

"Ah, puny master !" I cried in my delight,
   " Behold this gory holocaust and nameless !
   Why dost thou strike me not as I stand shameless?
Tell me, where is Thy might ?

" Thy threats are impotent, oh, fallen one !
  Vain, ruthless god of chastisement and error,
  I scorn Thee as a worm that writhes in terror !
Mark what my hand hath done !

" Of hideous work, Jehovah most austere !
  This is alone the terrible beginning !
  All upon Earth, the innocent, the sinning,
By me shall disappear !

" Thou art the slave of man born to obey
  Before the tempest of my wrath indignant,
  And now imperiously, oh God, malignant !
I bid Thee go Thy way !

" No lips again will Thy false name adore ;
  Thy power most irredeemably is broken.
  Bow down before me, for I, man, have spoken ;
There will be life no more !"

And as I spake the law of my desire,
  Wind-like I sped in fierce exasperation,
  Filled with red visions of extermination,
To slay my sons and sire !

But pains mysterious, and by me unknown,
  Clung to my loins ; I felt my pulses quicken,
  And, by the laggard hand of God, I, stricken,
Upon the ground fell prone.

Conscious of lofty projects overcast,
  I lay frenetic, crushed, inefficacious,
  Feeling that my sublimest dream audacious
Had unto nothing passed.

     *   *   *   *   *   *

God bade me rise, and on my brow did place
  A hated mark, whereby all mortals know me,
  By which a child unto a child can show me,
An odium, a disgrace !

Then to the land of Nod upon the plain,
  An outcast, but impenitent, He sent me,
  There to know agony and to repent me
In unattended pain.

I went rebellious with my treasured hate,
  And sullen through the desert now I wander,
  But when upon my mighty dreams I ponder,
I know that they were great !

POTIPHAR'S WIFE.

In dreams serene I saw before me rise,
Fertile and fragrant, by the lake-winds fanned,
Delicious vistas of the Holy Land,
Where Ephraim's vales in verdant grace expand
  Their hallowed beauty to the ravished eyes.

Gerizim reared in air its lofty height,
A gleaming maze of olive boughs and flowers,
Guarding the crumbled mold of Roman towers ;
While, in its majesty of barren bowers,
  Grim Ebal brooded in the Syrian night.

Between each rugged base, in starry gloom,
My wandering gaze by mystic power was led
Unto a mound, with vines and wild buds spread,
The sanctuary of immortal dead,
  The spot all-holy which is Joseph's tomb.

And as I wondered, in religious awe,
Before the dust of that great patriarch, dear
To Hebrew hearts, who, piously austere,
Bearded the sullen Pharaoh without fear,
  Musing upon his blameless life, I saw

A dolorous ghost, that, uttering low sighs,
Crept near the tomb, as if in timid quest,
A homeless spirit, tortured with unrest,
By some sublime fatality oppressed,
  With haggard cheeks, with vague, imploring eyes.

Marveling and mute, I dared not then demand
Whence she had come, or how, but I could trace
All Egypt's beauty blooming in her face,
While, with a sudden weird and ghastly grace,
  She clasped a mantle in one shadowy hand.

Its folds she wound about her like a shroud,
And tangled them amid her dusky hair,
Then paused and knelt in agonized despair
Before the sacred mound, and all the air
  Was still, while in her grief she cried aloud:

"Oh Joseph! most beloved and chosen one !
Can not long centuries of tears assuage
Thy heartless rancor toward me?   Can thy rage
Last longer than my misery?   Oh sage,
　　Oh lover, prophet, what thing have I done

"To feel, alas! thy everlasting scorn?
Must it eternal through the ages grow?
Hast thou no pity for my desperate woe,
When for a million eves I bend below
　　The potals of thy callous grave to mourn?

"Must I forever in the winter chill,
And sultry summer, answerless implore
Thy pardon for a wrong that is no more,
Alas! when 1 most ardently adore
　　Thy vanished beauty and thy memory still?

"Have no soft sounds of lamentations mine
The injury of the cruel past effaced?
Am I in thy pure soul for time disgraced?
Oh, man relentless, phantom sadly chaste,
　　Art thou in death than on earth more divine?

"See! thy fair mantle in my hand I hold,
A shred of thee, as sacred as thy kiss,
Far holier than the heart of Anubis,
And, though the joys of Paradise I miss,
    Still have I clung to it as worlds grow old!

"Oh Joseph! though I suffer for thee here,
My pain is sweet, and all the pangs thereof!
What raptures could I gain in spheres above,
Greater than my sad, unrequited love,
    That lives while stars are born and disappear?

"And yet, oh luminous promise of my soul,
If thou shouldst waken from thy tranquil sleep,
Which seraphim with holy vigils keep,
Reward my trust, unfalteringly deep,
    And speak *one* word, I will have gained my goal!

"Recall the languorous and ecstatic days,
When first I feasted eyes upon thy charms!
How could I spurn, with virtuous alarms,
The sinewy splendor of thy robust arms,
    Thy god-like brow, and thine alluring ways?

"Wast thou not fair and beautiful, while he,
Swart Potiphar, my husband and my lord,
Awed by the leaping terror of his sword
And jealous brows?   Ah, love could ill afford
   To spurn for him the excellence of thee !

"Blame for my sin, if sin it be, alone,
The curves symmetric of thy perfect limbs ;
Blame the grave music of Hebraic hymns,
The memory of thy voice that nothing dims ;
   Blame my frail heart that could not be of stone.

"Blame the voluptuous murmur of the Nile,
The pomp and glitter of thy home, the palm
That shaded every revery, the calm
Of torrid star-thronged nights, the gentle balm
   Of dreamy wines, but, above all, thy smile!

"Ah, how could I of fervent flesh resist
The tingling festivals of mad desire
That held sweet riot in ,me, with a fire
That scorned Osiris and the mage's ire,
   When, bold, I languished for thy lips unkissed ?

"Greater to me than Phthas' gemmed glories were
The nubile, supple graces of thy form!
Could I dispel swift hankerings that swarm,
When nerves are palpitant, and blood is warm?
    Could I gaze on thy wonder and not err?

"Oh Joseph! hear me ere I hasten hence!
The drowsy night is failing in the west;
Quell the sad torment of my harrowed breast,
If thou hast mercy; I have all confessed;
    Grand child of God, grant me my recompense!"

*   *   *   *   *   *

Then in the vague, gray gloaming I could see
The poor, unpardoned ghost caress the mound,
Where envied pity she had never found,
Prostrate and humble on the leafy ground,
    Clutching the mantle in dumb agony!

And when her lamentations seemed to cease,
To this distracted spirit, love-denied,
A dull, sepulchral voice at last replied,
And from the crypt's deep gloom in anger cried:
    "Away, thou specter harlot, give me peace!"

A SOUL'S SOLILOQUY.

Soul of a Sleeping Man Speaks.

Life holds for me no future joy or sweetness,
  My lofty mission here below has failed,
  And my prayer's purity has not availed
To change the odium of my incompleteness ;
    No power above
     Will free me from the forces that enmesh
     My vital essence in this hateful flesh,
      Which I am doomed to love.

My strength untried, my burning will and splendor
  Must be forever crushed, despised and mute ;
  For I am caged within this nescient brute,
Who knows my value not, and I must render
    Respect and praise
     To his vile body, guard his useless breath,
     And serve him slavishly until his death,
      Through sad, eventless days !

The cruel God that I revered unjustly
  Chose me for this foul task from radiant spheres.
  I, who was formed of vague, extrinsic tears ;
I, atom of love that roamed through Heaven augustly ;
    I, pure, serene,
   Was bidden to leave His paradise, obey,
   And animate a mass of senseless clay,
    And blend with flesh unclean.

And when from mystic realms, with strange tuition,
  I with expectancy sublime had fled,
  A voice like moaning thunders to me said :
" Oh soul ! remember well thy sacred mission.
    To the unborn
   Give all thy passion, and with breath of flame
   Illume the darkness in that formless frame ;
    Turn chaos into morn ! "

And I obeyed. Alas ! my will, attendant
  On him for fruitless years, has striven in vain,
  Through anguish and ungovernable pain,
To make his name unto the world resplendent.

But his base mind
Rejects the proffered power at my command ;
My threats or prayers he can not understand ;
His eyes to me are blind !

False, arrogant and vile, my body wanders,
Sinful, redemptionless, through stupid life,
Lacking a virile courage for the strife,
Knowing me not, although my wealth it squanders,
While the dull years
Creep like a wounded snake unto the tomb,
While I, before inevitable doom,
Conscious, await in fears.

That loathsome being, now my lifelong prison,
Will nothing dare, atrocious or sublime !
The germs of virtue or the seeds of crime
Have never in his mongrel heart arisen,
And all the fires
That I inherit from my native sky
Fail to arouse his torpor ; he will die
Like his forgotten sires !

And even in death I shall not find elation ;
   No soothing hope can e'er remain for me
   When from his odious corpse I skyward flee,
And leave him, object of my desecration,
      In some vile tomb.
      His mottled carrion, hated and unblest,
      Like scores of others, will forever rest
         In obloquy and gloom.

And then, made free, through darkness dense and awful
   I must perpetually in torment roam,
   Bereft of any heaven, hope or home,
Such is God's fiat, cruel and unlawful,
      Without a goal,
      For his eventless, sluggish life of scorn
      I, in my feeble innocence, must mourn ;
         I, his sad, stricken soul !

But, did he do some deed sublime and glorious,
   Were he to die in some wild, startling way,
   Unlike the common herds of dross and clay,
Ah ! then, elect, superb, transformed, victorious,

His praises I would sing !
But what all-subtle power, when I have none,
Will murmur in his ear, " This should be done,"
And fire to ashes bring ?

Ah ! I would give, to quell this daily torment,
My immortality, were it not too late.
Crushed by the hand of some invisible fate,
My power to urge him lies inert and dormant.
Calm as the sky,
He will live on, this rigid sphinx of men,
Until Death's hounds bark in his heart, and then
In calm ways he will die !

Oh ! I would fawn in lowly ways before him,
Could he on fierce inquisitorial pyres,
A heretic, be burned in sulphurous fires,
And see the horrid heat-waves circle o'er him.
Then I could soar
Forth from his charred and crackling, quivering flesh,
And, resurrect, be beautiful and fresh
Above the fagots' roar !

For some wild, bizarre death I crave and languish,
 Ere his dull, unimportant days are spent!
 Fierce joy 't would lend me, and unique content,
Could I but hear him in atrocious anguish,
  As in my dreams,
  Shriek madly unto God when courage failed,
  A sickening mass of horror, steel-impaled,
   Where haughty Stamboul gleams!

Is there no fate supreme and beatific,
 Although I suffer in his every throe,
 Which in some sea, when tempests moan their woe,
Could drag him downward in dismay terrific,
  Full of mad murmurings,
  When, as he struggled in a hell of foam,
  I could leap from him and regain my home
   With glad, white wings?

No! I am doomed, and yet, though hope is meager,
 I fain would lure him where some famished beast
 In the miasmal jungles of the east
Might loom before him truculent and eager!

Or with my hates
Lead his poor, timorous feet in utter dread
Among rank ferns and reeking grass to tread
Where some damp cobra waits !

Oh God, be merciful !   The days pass faster !
Hope dies within me, and my wings are cold ;
He whom I loathe is growing blind and old ;
The dreaded time has come of my disaster ;
Oh, God of might !
In pity strike him with thy lightning dire,
Although I perish in its livid fire
And be naught in the night !

EMBARRASSMENT.

Gaunt wreckers watch the wintry coast at night;
 The tempest rages in the outward gloom;
 Rough men are praying unto God to doom
A vessel struggling with the ocean's might.

Crowded and kneeling in supreme affright
 Upon the fated ship, a floating tomb,
 Vast, helpless throngs are seen when lightnings lume,
Beseeching God for salvatory light!

And He in highest Heaven doth hear these prayers
 Offered by every soul with voice sincere,
  Who for his sentence in distraction waits,
And He, environed by a million cares,
 Looks on the scene of triumph and of fear,
  Uplifts his judging hand, and—hesitates!

SAMSON AND DELILAH.

Now Samson issued from the tribe of Dan,
And by his sire Manoah, a righteous man,
  Was loved, ere born, by heavenly prediction ;
    For unto him the Angel of the Lord
    Appeared, and with the waving of a sword
  Had banished from his tent all doubts' affliction.

And Samson thrived amid his father's herds,
Alone with them and the wild forest birds,
  And he waxed strong, from merry wine abstaining,
    Obedient to his Nazaritish vow ;
    For the Lord's benediction on his brow
  In ways propitious was beheld remaining.

And it so happened that no warrior then,
No valorous leader of a thousand men,
  Ever by taunt or daring tone incensed him ;
    But once, while dreaming of his untried strength,
    Stretching his knotted arms their massive length,
  A young impetuous lion roared against him.

Then, lo! the spirit of the living Lord
Aroused him from the green snare of the sward,
  And lightning-like came mightily upon him,
    . And towering, with resistless power he rent
      The clamorous beast asunder by his tent,
  As though he were a reed, and trampled on him !

And it so happened and so came to pass,
He seized the ponderous jaw-bone of an ass,
  When by Philistine hosts environed densely,
    And with the thunder of his battle-cry,
    Did smite the sudden assailants hip and thigh,
  Until the ground with death was dark intensely.

Now, by such deeds of valor and renown,
Samson was feared in the Philistine town,
  Where he in haughty unconcern would wander,
    Pacing with chosen paranymphs the street,
    And with the fairest woman he chanced to meet
  Would sup and lavishly his manch squander.

For Samson, while he brooded in dull ease,
Was strongly moved by passion's mysteries ;
  His virgin heart craved sympathies unnumbered,

And the imperious, devastating flame
Of great desires held their allegiant frame,
Or in his rebel sinews lightly slumbered.

Now there dwelt within the Sorek vale
A harlot named Delilah, lithe and pale,
With starry eyes and silver-studded tresses,
Who, dyed with herbs, paced the broad, peopled ways,
Dancing, or singing Midianitish lays,
Selling the fever of her warm caresses.

And she had longed for one enamored hour
With Samson, radiant in his nubile power;
Languished and dreamed to win him and inspire
His bones with palpitations of delight,
And through the dreamy silences of night
To fill his veins with all-consuming fire!

But he had spurned her beauty in its bloom
For rosy Tinnah, in the woodland's gloom,
Ay, on her lighted threshold had he scorned her;
Ay! though the spice and perfume of the east
Her supple, naked loveliness increased;
Ay! though her pearls and amulets adorned her.

And dull hate for the spurner moved her breast ;
His calm indifference, cruelly expressed,
    Turned to foul gall her wakening senses maddened,
        And to draw harm's disaster on his head,
        To cause him pain, or see his valor dead,
    Her proud, vindictive spirit would have gladdened.

Now, once it happened at patrician feast,
When mirth in ways unhallowéd increased,
    Delilah, on the strong man's cushion seated,
        Drugged the spiced food, and Samson, love-entranced,
        Upon the charms he had forsaken glanced,
    Laughed in his beard, and wooed her, and entreated.

Therefore unto her home she lured him, where
Wrapt in the perfumed mantle of her hair,
    He lay in languid love's divine prostration,
        Moved to his mighty soul by love's excess
        And all the roses of her loveliness,
    Kissing her eyes in silent adoration.

But while in troubled ravishment he slept,
The alert Philistine haters near him crept,
    With glittering bribes down laden, to discover

The mystery that filled their souls with awe,
And by her lecherous sorcery to draw
The dreaded secret from her dreamy lover.

But, flushed by soft excesses and her hate,
Nude and disheveled, then she bade them wait,
With promises, until the hour propitious,
And with the silver pieces given, returned
Where Samson lingered, and in revery burned,
To taste again her shameless kiss delicious.

And, lo! it happened that her Samson came,
Proud neophyte of love, once more to claim
Of her embraces the delicious honey,
And with him, in youth's exaltation, brought
Tunics and veils by skillful fingers wrought,
Brilliant with gems and burdened with much money.

And she said to him : " Tell me, little sun,
Sweet, sun-like Samson, pray what might be done
To tame thy lion strength, oh, radiant giant?
Tell me, I beg of thee!" And he did speak :
"Bind me with withes, and then shall I be weak,
Ay, like a lamb, most pitiful and pliant."

So when he slept, she bound him, and she called
Unto her cringing acolytes appalled :
  "Behold ! the man is bound and slaved by slumbers."
    But, as they crept upon him, he arose,
    Shook off the shackle of sleep and with sharp blows
  Fell on them there and slew them in great numbers.

And pale Delilah in her anger cried :
"Behold ! thou much hast mocked me and hast lied !
  Tell me then freest truth that I may cherish !"
    And Samson said : "Oh, summer of my hopes,
    If I be bounden with unsullied ropes,
  Then will my boasted valor wane and perish."

Again on her exultant breast he slept ;
Again the eager chieftains toward him crept ;
  By dire distrust and coward fancies shaken,
    Seeing him helpless in his dormant pride,
    While with alarming voice, Delilah cried :
  "Philistines are upon thee, Samson ! Waken !"

And he leapt forth in wonderment and wrath,
Sweeping through shields a desolating path,
  Cleaving the serried ranks like flax asunder,

And o'er the clashing armor of his foes,
Above the slaughter and the fury, rose
His clarion voice, defiant, like a thunder !

But hate had made Delilah's spirit strong,
And with her jests she lashed as with a thong
His patience, till he cried in indignation :
"If I should lose my flowing locks, ah ! then
Indeed shall I be like all other men,
Of equal might in strength and emulation !"

Then multitudes of angered warriors came
To seize the hostage of Delilah's shame,
For with sly cunning she had caught and taken
The rough and tangled forest of his hair,
And Samson, all unmanned, lay pinioned there,
And was by the Almighty Lord forsaken.

Nerveless and mute with grief, they dragged their prize
Up to the town, and burned his haughty eyes,
Proud of his sullen, utter desolation,
Laughing to see the phantom of their dread
Unto the prison by a stripling led,
Glad of his woe and hideous hesitation.

The angry populace clamored for his life,
And many a javelin and glittering knife
    Flashed danger in the phalanxes around him,
        But he was doomed to be the people's slave,
        Unworthy of the solace of a grave,
    And with huge fetters of strong brass they bound him.

Now, as the days in slow procession passed,
His mutilated locks grew long at last,
    And with them dawned again his virile splendor,
        And, in unspeakable distress he prayed
        Unto Jehovah for celestial aid
    To smite the intolerant pride of his offender.

And it so happened that Philistine hordes
Gathered together full a thousand swords
    To offer savory sacrifice to Dagon,
        A hideous image, a bejeweled clod,
        Who of their sinful destinies was god,
    And who was worshiped by the rabble pagan.

And loud within his temple did they come,
Rejoicing with the timbrel and the drum,
    While minnims and melodious sabecs quivered,

Praising the high, commandant god whose power
Had saved the nation in its sorest hour,
And who to them had such a foe delivered.

And when their hearts were gladdened by strong wine,
They bade Delilah with a haughty sign
  Seek shackled Samson, in his prison stricken,
    And by his monstrous helplessness to make
    Exciting sport of him for Dagon's sake,
  And with derisive jibes their pleasures quicken.

So she, Delilah, servant unto this,
Came unto Samson with a traitress kiss,
  And of their sovereign commandment told him ;
    Thus, once again, leading the cruel way,
    Her irritating arm upon him lay,
  Ay, one spell more did her soft arms enfold him.

And he spoke to her : " Oh, Delilah, sweet !
I pray thee linger at my weary feet ;
  Remember my past love and have this pity."
    And, as he murmured, crushed by his despair,
    Exultant laughter shook the perfumed air,
  Re-echoing at the gates and in the city.

And he was placed, with curses and hard blows,
Between two mighty pillars that arose
  High to the domes, and false Delilah near him
    Agged his distress with languid serpent words,
    While the wine-laden lords in boisterous herds
  Taunted his weaknesses and failed to fear him.

Then Samson, in a tumult of despair,
Bent low his brows in majesty of prayer,
  And called unto the Lord in his prostration :
    "Great God sublime, who madest the green earth,
    Whose will omnipotent hath given me birth,
  Eternal God of infinite creation !

"Remember me, I pray, oh Holy One !
Forgive, forget the wrongs my hands have done !
  Strengthen this faltering arm that would obey Thee !
    Strengthen this wretched clay that worships Thee !
    Strengthen my soul that hungers to be free !
  Receive it, oh omniscient God ! I pray Thee ! "

Then he arose and, comforted, he cried :
"Delilah, oh Delilah ! thou hast lied ;
  Thou, of this hated race the boldest harlot !

It was thy kiss that lured me to this doom,

It was thy flower-breath that hath made my tomb,

Ay, 'twas thy beauty robed in vexing scarlet !

"'Twas thy gold flood of tresses steeped in spice,

Thy lying lips, thy warm breasts that entice,

That led me from the solitude I cherish.

Thou, thou alone, with thy god-tempting face,

Hast brought me to disaster and disgrace !

Pray *now* ! pray, pray, even *now*, for thou shalt perish !"

And then he bowed himself with all his might

Between the mammoth pillars, and the sight

Filled with fast fear the thousand there assembled.

"Receive my soul, oh God !" he loudly cried,

While the vast temple cracked from side to side,

And the great dome with ominous thunder trembled.

Then down from dizzy height the ponderous weight

Fell on the doomed Philistines of his hate ;

Fell on the men whom God to him delivered,

And in the gloom, the horror and dismay,

Crushed by his side the false Delilah lay,

While at her bleeding throat his hand still quivered !

April, 1881.

WORSHIP.

I, faithful, can not in a God believe
　Who in majestic ways will be revered,
　When I am dead and shall have disappeared,
Before whose altars men unborn will grieve.

To *my* God giving, from Him I would receive,
　I being in jealous moods and fashions reared,
　And crave to pray to One divinely feared,
One unto whom, when timorous, I can cleave.

If such be worshiped by the common throng,
　To me It is not God, for I desire
　　Some Thing immense, omnipotent, alone,
Some Vagueness nameless in my feeble song ;
　Some Power of splendor, fury and of fire,
　　Some mystic wonder to the world unknown

1879.

GOD'S ENNUI.

I am the Lord and Master over all ;
   In me the essence of creation lies ;
   I *will*, and from dim chaos life will rise ;
The comets at my bidding pass or fall.

I awe the timid spheres ; my whims appall
   The wondering stars that beautify the skies,
   And the dull insect, man, who cowers and cries
Upon the earth, gives homage at my call.

But weary of my unquestioned powers I grow,
   Feeling at times that I could gladly see
      The worlds I have created swoon and fade,
Annihilated by a single blow ;
   And then again I often long to be
      The lowliest worm that I have ever made !

June, 1880.

DISCONTENT.

Roses may weary of their suave, rare scent ;
   If the apparent azure of the sky
   Were really fair, would white clouds hurry by?
The songs of birds may be for Death's ear meant.

The brook perchance may moan its discontent,
   And tremulous leaves wave litanies, to try
   In these mute ways to move the power on high,
And by such sad appeal make God relent !

If Nature grieves, supremely unsatisfied,
   Waiting in vain the paradise of decay,
     I will not in life's desert, seeing this wrong,
Spaniel to unjust powers and please their pride,
   Having no heart to sing their praise alway,
     I, who am crushed, poor Ishmael of song !

CURIOSITY.

The patient stars that, luminously strong,
   Lavished on earth their sad, reluctant light,
   The sullen sun doomed to be ever bright,
The weary moon we rhapsodize in song,

Will cry aloud some day : " What unknown wrong
   Have we committed in Thy august sight,
   Oh God most just, omnipotent and right?
How long must we now serve Thee, ay, how long?

" We weary of the ceaseless flow of years
   That bring no change, and we are fain to die,
     Born with the essence of the faith that saves."
Then, echoing through the voids of endless space,
   A hollow voice of thunders will reply :
     " Peace, wretched atoms, know that ye are slaves !"

JUDAS.

Once, when with fever of unrest I slumbered,
    Wearied by shadowy fancies without aim,
Uncertain dreams and vague alarms unnumbered,
    Before mine eyes there came

The semblance of a spirit most mysterious,
    A presence whose approaching breath was warm,
A shape that stood before me, stern and serious,
    Taking a human form.

Its lofty brow seemed seared by sin's excesses ;
    A deathly pallor blanched a haggard face,
While supplicating eyes beneath long tresses
    Lighted the brow's disgrace.

Yet in its troubled gaze was purely shining
    A consciousness of undisputed right,
Suffering perchance beyond all earth's divining,
    But fearless of the light.

The misty shadow silently drew near me.
   And, while in fear tumultuous I stirred,
It whispered gently : " Nay, do thou not fear me,
     But hearken to my word.

" I, a despised and deeply injured spirit,
   Who ne'er of justice have beheld the ruth,
Who upon earth man's deathless hate inherit,
     Come to reveal *the truth*.

" Races and worlds by death are urned and embered,
   Since, living, Judah has shuddered at my name,
And it, alas ! is even to-day remembered
     With loathing and with shame !

" I have been wronged with perfidy infernal,
   And none have dared my memory to defend,
And, through dead centuries that seemed eternal,
     On earth I found no friend.

" For I am *Judas*, the presumptive traitor !
   But shrink not for thy virtues so unpriced ;
I come as humble supplicant, not as hater,
     I, who sold Jesus Christ !

"I come to thee, not as I am in spirit,
 But with the odious form on earth once mine,
Not as the clod who can all feuds inherit,
 But Judas *the Divine!*

"Ay! and with these thrice pardoned lips to tell thee
 The story of my infamy and wrong,
And the attentive world will not repel thee,
 If thou art pure and strong.

"For I am guiltless of the dire disaster
 By which all-holy Christ to doom was led;
I purely worshiped my immortal master;
 For Him I would have bled.

"I loved his words, that made my spirit sweeter;
 My soul was free from any taint of guile;
I was the brother and the friend of Peter,
 And lived in Jesus' smile!

"I, the poor Kerioth sinner, beggar, dreamer,
 Had gained, oh envied goal! his hallowed love,
Than love of shining seraphim supremer,
 Love purer than a dove!

" For I was happy in the vales Judean,
   Where one and all his gentle glance could claim,
And when I hearkened to the ceaseless pæan
    That hailed his august name,

" When we together walked by joys elated,
   That even no sad, ulterior torment mars,
'While over us his blue home scintillated
    With majesties of stars !

" And where he told us of the Heavenly wonders
   Which we, if pure of spirit, would behold,
How we should hear God's grand, melodious thunders
    In radiant towns of gold !

" And I recall his allegories tender,
   How we should mutely suffer for God's sake,
While the Samarian moon in flawless splendor
    Haloed the murmuring lake.

" Ay ! and my whole soul with a rapture nameless
   Yearned to make perilless his wandering life.
And save the Son of God, alone and blameless,
    From outrage and all strife.

"In those most consecrated days, oh mortal!
 In those indelible and perfect hours,
To heal the stricken at the city's portal,
  I had my Master's powers!

"Ay, the rare boon unto my brothers given,
 To combat pain, to comfort, to allay,
To heal the maimed, when all in vain had striven,
  And send them on their way!

"And more, oh man! I was so greatly cherished
 That Christ the common purse unto me gave,
To aid the poor who on the high roads perished,
  To fortify, to save.

"And thus o'er fruitful valley lands we wandered,
 Through bastioned towns and desert wastes of sand,
While at each step the Savior paused and pondered,
  Blessing the favored land.

"But ah! there came a day of doom impendent
 To me, in strangest manner unforeseen,
When first I saw in loveliness transcendent
  Mary, the Magdalene!

" Her loosened tresses in their uncurbed splendor,
A stream of gold like ripe and wavy wheat,
Fell o'er her bosom palpitant and tender
To kiss her sandaled feet.

" And the soft eyes whose mutable effulgence
Caused my dumb heart to flutter in surprise,
Filled with all mercy and with all indulgence,
Were like my Master's eyes !

" And I adored her in my uncouth fashion,
And wooed her love with all my love new-born,
With timid questionings, with ardent passion,
With heart and bosom torn.

" And her mute answer to my prayer ambitious
Thrilled me with rapture's all-consuming flame,
While from her lips, oh, ecstasy delicious !
The sweet avowal came !

" And then, impatient, urged by fears mysterious,
I long implored her on my bended knee
To cross the wavy darkness of Tiberias,
And make her tent with me.

(7)

"And she, to every whim conceived, consented,
    Ay ! to all plans my fevered fancy drew,
But I was poor, and grievously lamented,
      Knowing not what to do.

"Ah then, O man, from no chagrin exempted,
    Blind by my passion, scourged by passion's rod,
I, by the Lord omnipotent was tempted,
      Ay, by the living God !

"He came unto me in my sad prostration
    And cried : ' *Iscariot, hearken and obey !*
If thou aspirest to thy soul's salvation,
      Jesus thou must betray !

"' *Here will thou suffer in the hopes thou leadest,*
    Here wilt thy life be piteous to foretell,
But if my most supreme command thou heedest,
      In heaven thy soul shall dwell ! '

"And then with this omniscient will superior
    I struggled while I walked and while I slept,
Growing by doubts and passion each day wearier,
      Ay, wearier, as I wept !

" ' Surely ! ' I cried, bewildered, ' oh ! most surely
    God hath ordained to try my soul undone;
He will protect my Christ who slumbers purely,
        Jesus, who is His son !

" ' I can obey Him, gaining sweet salvation,
    And fly with radiant Mary unalarmed,
While God will strengthen Him in His probation,
        And leave His soul unharmed ! '

" This I resolved that day of dire disaster,
    When walking with my brethren, side by side,
I went to sup with my beloved Master,
        And sat me by His side.

" And he spake to us, when we were assembled:
    ' One of you present will betray me here ! '
And then I murmured gladly, though I trembled:
        ' He knows and hath no fear !

" ' He has divined my thought, and knows Jehovah
    Has chosen me now His wishes to obey;
He knows His father's mandate, and moreover
        That I am to betray !

" ' And, when the deed is done, He, on the foemen,
    Who dread His holihead with nameless dread,
Ay, on the cohorts and the rabble Roman,
        Will nameless terror spread ! '

" My heart grew firmer; I could doubt no longer;
    My tortured soul found infinite content,
And to the grave Sanhedrim, calmer, stronger,
        With hurried steps I went.

" And there I asked : ' What sum will ye give to me,
    If I deliver and hand unto you
My Master, who hath chosen to pursue me,
        My Master, Christ, the Jew ?'

" And they together, in hushed exultation,
    Did covenant with me in silent shame
For thirty silver pieces of the nation,
        If I should do that same.

" And my sad, timorous soul awoke delighted ;
    Peace, peace had lulled its tempest at the last ;
I saw the daring future unaffrighted ;
        My doubts, my dreams were past !

" And strengthened by fair Hope's restoring manna,
   Seeing the world more beautiful and fair,
I hurried forth with many a glad hosanna
     To meet my Mary there !

" Amid a tumult of delight I told her
   That night to await me in a secret place,
And was exalted, purified, made bolder
     By her divine embrace.

" Then from the town than hunted camels faster,
   To Kedron's brook, free from perplexing care,
I followed secretly my pensive Master,
     And saw Him kneel in prayer.

" Ay ! I, the aspiring Jew, the sad fanatic,
   Witnessed the holy silence of the place,
While the attendant moon with beams ecstatic
     Silvered His upturned face !

" And by me through the forest-tangles guided
   Came eager hundreds of his enemies,
Cravens and priests, who had His word derided,
     Elders and Pharisees !

" Officers, hurried from the Temple's porches,
　　Hirelings, with staves made ready to assail,
Soldiers, with flashing swords, and spears, and torches,
　　Soldiers of Rome in mail !

" And low they whispered:　' Traitor, we have missed
　　　　him !
No such a one as Christ has sought this dell !'
But I cried out:　' Hail Master !' and I kissed Him ;
　　Then upon Him they fell !

" And He said: 'Wherefore dost thou now betray me,
　　Oh, Judas, my disciple above all ?
Why did my watchful brethren not delay me,
　　Or answer to my call ?'

" And I said to Him :　' Was not this predicted ?
　　Didst thou not know thy Heavenly Father's will ?
Why in this hour of *power* standst thou afflicted ?'
　　And His white lips were still !

" But ah ! He gazed a moment strangely on me,
　　A look of wonder, pity and dismay,
And with averted eyes that seemed to shun me,
　　He then was led away.

"So unto me came Andrew, Jude and Thomas,
  Urging me then to leave the sullied spot,
For priests had given them sacerdotal promise,
    That they would harm Him not.

"And, being assured their council diabolic
  Would be frustrated by the guarding Lord,
Knowing Christ sacred, pure and apostolic,
    I left the desolate sward.

"Still marveling at the wonderful enigma,
  My body a fire, my brain a seething mist,
But freed by God's own word from any stigma,
    I hastened to the tryst,

"And then my vision, my doubt, my deed narrated,
  To radiant Mary in all haste's alarm,
And, by impatient longings enervated,
    Seized her reluctant arm.

"But she in anger and great wrath, indignant
  Cried : 'Christ, thy friend, my Savior and my goal,
Did hurl from me vile hosts of fiends malignant,
    And purified my soul !

"'I love Him in His pride and in disaster,
  I love the very pebbles he has trod,
I love Him as a man and as a master,
    I love Him as my God!

"'I lied, I lied to thee, oh Hell's own traitor!
  When to my lips the words of passion came;
I love Him as a lover; as a hater
    I hate thee and thy shame!

"'He said to me: "Thy sins are all forgiven!"
  He said to thee: "Judas, thou wilt betray!"
And now, destroyer, from all mercy driven,
    Away! Away! Away!'

"Frenzy, remorse, delirium satanic
  Possessed me in my infamous despair;
I knew naught, as my pulses throbbed in panic;
    I raved and rent my hair!

"And then, oh sacrifice most superhuman!
  I shrieked aloud, oblivious to her hate:
'Oh Mary, Mary Magdalen! oh woman!
    It is not yet too late!

"'Swear unto me by all thou holdest holy,
　By God's august, impenetrable brow,
That thou wilt follow me and be mine solely,
　　And I will save Christ now.'

"And she gasped : 'Go, and here will I await thee,
　But none can know how my poor heart will bleed,
Nor how my outraged womanhood can hate thee
　　For this, thy foulest deed !'

"Then to the stern Sanhedrim, panting, livid,
　I flew, nor did my tireless effort cease
Until, with loud appealing voice and vivid,
　　I begged the Lord's release.

"And oh ! the anguish of atonement's sorrow !
　None then would listen to my frantic cries ;
No sympathy, no justice could I borrow
　　By menaces or sighs.

"And maddened by their answers emblematic,
　With indignation and despair I burst,
And cried aloud in threatening tones emphatic :
　　'Take back your coin accursed !

"' I will not keep this silver foul and tainted ;
   The barter of my conscience is unpriced ;
I see my sin ! I have betrayed my sainted,
      All-holy Master, Christ !

"' But ye, who fear His parables pacific,
   His holy teachings that can never die,
Ye, who reject His godhead beatific,
      Are wretcheder than I ! '

" And then I ceased to blame them or implore them,
   While they gazed on me in sore disarray,
But hurled the shining pieces down before them,
      And turned my feet away.

" Unarmed and crushed, and scorning even pity,
   Calmly to waiting Mary I did go,
While she, in anguish clamoring, sought the city,
      And left me to my woe.

" And as I wandered, desolate, pathetic,
   Alone on earth, without a love or tie,
I cried : ' Oh God ! recall thy words prophetic !
      I am about to die ! '

"And where, in glory, near the calm lake glowing,
    The mellow moon most radiantly shone,
I chanced upon a fig-tree thereby growing,
    And hanged myself thereon !

  *   *   *   *   *   *

"Now learn, oh man ! that after I had perished,
    I suffered for all previous sinning done,
Like other men who sin, but I am cherished
    And pardoned for this one !

"It was God's will, and I, His slave, obeyed it.
    It was His stern commandment ; I obeyed.
It was His wish, and I was called to aid it,
    And I did give my aid.

"Tell unto men that I am no deceiver ;
    Tell them my wrong, my pardon and my pain,
And, as thou art no more my unbeliever,
    Purge my good name from stain !"

  *   *   *   *   *   *

Then in my dream, from which all doubt was banished,
    The phantom upward slowly seemed to soar,
And with a smile ineffable it vanished,
    And it was seen no more.

But as I shuddered in supremest terror,
And while still marveling and mute I lay,
Persuaded of my fancy's awful error,
I heard Iscariot say :

" Friend, I am now beyond the earth's affliction ;
I speak unto thee from a heavenly strand,
While Christ, our Savior, gives me benediction,
And, smiling, holds my hand ! "

April, 1881.

MOSES ON SINAI.

A Woman Speaks.

And Aaron said unto them : Break off the golden ear-rings of your
wives and of your daughters, and bring them unto me.—*Exodus xxxii: 2.*

Forth unto Horeb in my mighty sorrow
  I hastened, seeking everywhere the bland,
  Calm face of Moses, absent from the land
Now forty days, and from his laws to borrow
  Justice, and speedy vengeance from his hand ;

Moses, who walked to meet his awful Master,
  Alone among dull thunders, face to face,
  He who could give me fortitude and grace
To bear the burden of my fell disaster,
  He who could crush the haughty and the base.

And forth o'er crags granitic to entreat him
  I went, with blurred eyes and disheveled hair,
  Goaded by all the serpents of despair,
Yet knowing not if I should chance to meet him,
  High in the mountains, lost in saintly prayer.

But where the misty and rugged cliffs had ending,
  Fresh from the look of God, erect and white,
  And most exultant by His sound and sight,
I saw his venerable form descending
  With sere brows haloed in seraphic light.

The glory of the unknown was on him beaming,
  Safe from the mystery whose name alarms,
  Safe from the terror of malignant harms,
And as he came upon me, pale and dreaming,
  He held two tablets in his withered arms.

Filled with sublimest awe and inspiration,
  He gazed upon me with bewildered eyes,
  On me, the interruption, the surprise !
But in the torment of my desolation
  I heeded not, and, fearless, spake this wise :

"Oh Moses ! my hushed wrongs can stay no longer !
  Oh most revered one ! harken to my plea !
  Before thy matchless majesty my knee
Bends down, but now my hardiness grows stronger.
  Oh, Moses ! Moses ! harken unto me !

" Know, I am Helia, for thou canst not know me,
    A woman of the Levi tribe, distressed,
    And by thy brother, Aaron, sore oppressed.
Oh, grand justiciary of our people ! show me
    Thy law and light, and honor my behest !

" To call on thee I have not hesitated
    Up Sinai's hollow fastnesses to plod.
    I have sought thee in the presence of thy God,
And, daring all, to beg thee venerated,,
    To smite and chastise Israel with thy rod.

"While thou wast absent in these wilds ferocious,
    Know that the thousands in thy care have spurned
    The living God, and have with anthems turned
To worship idols bestial and atrocious,
    And for false gods have insolently burned.

" His altars are cast down !   They love another,
    A heavy clod of senseless, speechless gold !
    The wolves are many in Jehovah's fold,
And every heart by thine irreverent brother
    To misery and damnation has been sold.

"Thy impious Aaron who from duty falters,
  The pagan Levite, the anointed priest,
  In orgy obscene and many a loathesome feast
Hails Apis now, and Mnevis, on thine altars,
  And sacrifices to them herb and beast.

"By stern decrees implacable and cruel,
  By threats and awful glitterings of glaives, ,
  He has compelled us all, the free, the slaves,
To render up our every golden jewel ;
  Our wealth and hoardings the new fiend-god craves.

"Oh Moses, redolent of God ! molested
  By my weak cries, listen ! Thy brother said:
  'Let all the rings and all the bracelets, spread
Through Israel, from the men and maids be wrested
  To form an image mighty and hallowéd !'

"And oh ! my precious rings were taken from me,
  My darling jewels, yea, dearer than mine eyes,
  Although I filled the camp with claims and cries ;
Foul Aaron's hirelings strove to overcome me
  And tore from out mine ears the bleeding prize,

" The priceless gift of my sweet lover cherished,
  The pledge and cunning handiwork, alas !
  Of him who engraved the tabernacle's brass,
Its gold and silver, which ere now have perished,
  Doomed in the idol's sateless maw to pass !

" Bezaléel, he, than all the people wiser,
  The chosen of God, the wondersmith, whose art
  And beauty waved love's essence to my heart;
He, the miraculous and skilled deviser,
  Who toiled for God and not the common mart,

" My life and love rest in the rings he gave me !
  They were my all, *his* promise and *my* hope !
  Must I in pain unutterable grope ?
Oh, Moses ! from my dawning madness save me !
  Against my loss I can not, can not cope !

" Dearer were they to me, since he arrayed me
  Proudly in all the burnished charm thereof,
  Than future years of sweet, connubial love,
More than the child unborn that he has made me,
  More than the God who hears me from above.

(8)

" Yet he, my lover, flouts me and accuses
    My faithlessness with harsh, unfeeling tone ;
    He cries, deaf to my innocence alone :
' Helia ! thou soldst them gladly !' and refuses
    To call my love and body again his own.

" Why dost thou stand there, Moses, dumb and awful ?
    The God thou hast left will curse thy senile sneer !
    Wilt thou not answer me, grim man austere ?
Speak, moody patriarch !   Is thy silence lawful ?
    Thou dealst out justice ; *deal it to me here !*

" Oh, saintly insensate mortal, unimpassioned,
    I say to thee that Israel, gone astray,
    Is forced thy brother's mandates to obey,
And he, all-guilty, with his palms has fashioned
    A golden calf and worships it to-day !

" Thy nations bow before its glitter odious,
    They scoff at thee and thine eternal trust,
    And with degrading cries of mirth and lust
They hail it on soft lyres and lutes melodious,
    Dancing around it to thy God's disgust !"

Then as I foamed upon him, breathless, haggard,
  Moses the meek incredulously smiled,
  And said :   " Thou dreamest, woman most defiled !
By thee my faith fraternal is not staggered.
  Go, go thy way, poor maniac beguiled !

" Thy soul with vagrant fancies thou enslavest.
  Fare to the temple and thy God adore
  On humble knees, and all His grace implore.
If yet thou canst, go, woman, for now thou ravest."
  And, gazing upon his tablets, spake no more.

*   *   *   *   *   *

Then, in tumultuous, angered desperation,
  Incensed by such inflexible disdain,
  I clutched him, by my sorrow made insane,
And, with loud groans and sobs of indignation,
  I cursed his hoary beard and brows again.

And with the strength of multitudes in madness
  I dragged him up through sheer and rocky ways,
  Far on chill Sinai's summits, where they raise
High toward the stars, and, with a heart-felt gladness,
  I pointed down and bade the prophet gaze.

There, on the spacious plain, the sun descending
　　Flooded with lingering rays the impious throngs
　　Of Israel, who had wrought my woes and wrongs,
The Israel led from bondage, fiercely rending
　　The air with vile and sacrilegious songs !

There, in the fertile valley, had assembled
　　The noblest tribes, with twenty thousand tents,
　　To worship in their pagan insolence,
While, rising o'er the sea of heads that trembled,
　　The *Calf of Gold* gleamed in magnificence !

And Moses, seeïng it clearly, smote his forehead,
　　And, having scorned my warning word, the sage
　　Held high within his hands God's holy gage,
And, with anathemas severe and horrid,
　　Hurled down toward earth the tablets in his rage !

And, stammering, pale, his outraged spirit broken,
　　He stood and groaned his sorrow forth in sighs
　　That mingled with my loud, exulting cries,
While in an anguish left by man unspoken
　　The rebel tears gushed slowly from his eyes.

But I was unappeased and cried unto him,
  Glad of his misery : " Art thou yet content?
  Wilt thou believe me now, oh, prophet sent ?
Ah ! I demand thy brother's blood ; pursue him ;
  Give me the high priest's carrion, maimed and rent!"

And as I shrieked in throes of rage infernal,
  Upon the shattered tablets of my God,
  Lying in fragments on the holy sod,
Writ with the finger of the Lord eternal,
  I fearlessly and arrogantly trod !

" To me, oh Moses ! how can thy wrath matter ?
  Thou, aided by thy God, canst by a word
  Disperse and slay yon unrepenting herd,
And to the sands their bones felonious scatter,
  But I from vengeance ever am deterred !

" What moots it to me that thy faith is lost thee
  For one brief span ? God will not let thee fall ;
  Thy sudden advent will the camp appall,
The shadow of pain for one fleet hour has crossed thee ;
  Thou canst restore thy calm, but *I* lose all !

"*All! all!* for in that camp, I, chill and clamoring,
    Was seized and was despoiled of my rare worth,
    While Aaron watched me in contemptuous mirth,
And loudly scoffed my sobbing and my stammering,
    He the most despicably vile of earth!

"And there, bound tight with cords, cast down, rebelling,
    He forced me to that very altar's side,
    And made me worship my lost pledge and pride,
Fused with the rest, while in my bosom swelling
    His keen laugh pierced me, mute and terrified!

"Oh, Moses! Moses! let thy grave heart harden
    Toward these vile recreants, and their rites consume;
    Cast them to death, to torture and to gloom;
Tear from thy soul the fragile seeds of pardon.
    Moses! thy duty tells thee thou must doom!"

*   *   *   *   *   *

And Moses harkened to my objurgation;
    He calmed my wrath with benedictions rare;
    He pacified and blessed me with a prayer;
And we went down to stay the profanation,
    And Israel at our coming trembled there.

Upon the people castigations fearful
  Fell, and woe wandered swiftly through the land,
  And at the patriarch's supreme command
A thousand guilty heroes grew plagued and tearful,
  " For God did strike them with His mighty hand."

For Moses took the hated calf and burned it,
  And mixed therewith foul water till it stank,
  And though the tribes in loathing from it shrank,
Begging for grace, and irritated spurned it,
  The law was law, and stricken Israel drank.

Then through the camp each man in bloody labor
  Did slay his brother, and each brother slew
  His boon companion, smiting through and through,
And each companion smote his cherished neighbor,
  As it was fit, and as God bade them do !

And I, avenged by blood, in exultation
  Stood near to Moses, witness of this shame
  And righteous torture by the sword and flame
That fell upon this God-afflicted nation ;
  I saw it all, and found no word of blame.

Now in my tent, alone, but calm and cheerless,
Like some weak tigress that has lost its mate,
Brooding in tranquil ways upon my fate,
Most satisfied at heart, and very fearless,
The wrath of sullen Aaron I await!

AD SUMMUM DEUM.

If, oh God, thou art eternal,
Most omnipotent, supernal,
Spare us from life's pains diurnal !

Burning with doubt's torrid fever,
I, poor worm and unbeliver,
Ask of thee, supreme Deceiver,

Wherefore in such ways distress me ?
If thou art Jehovah, bless me,
Or with proofs of power impress me !

How can I respect thy glory,
When through years of myth and story
Thou appearest stern and gory ?

Can the throngs of souls, o'ertaken
By thy wrath, by thee forsaken,
Love and faith in men awaken ?

AD SUMMUM DEUM.

Can we call thee just and blameless,
When by thy desertion shameless
We still groan here blind and aimless?

If thy glory could attain to
Heights of pardon, and disdain to
Curse thy creatures who are fain to

Love thee in devotion artless,
Thou couldst make the wide world smartless,
God malignant, dumb and heartless!

For thy Son's divine prediction,
Must weak mortals in affliction
Wait another crucifixion?

Why, if he has died to spare us
From all torments, shouldst thou bear us
Hate implacable, and dare us

In our wretchedest prostration,
With thine anger's desolation?
Are we not of thy creation?

If the sun and stars thou makest,
If supreme the spheres thou shakest,
If from naught thou something takest,

Prove it to us, though thou rend us
In divine ways and tremendous.
Thrill us with thy might stupendous !

For we scorn thy clamorous thunder ;
When thou tearest clouds asunder,
We but smile and do not wonder.

Dost thou deem thy puny lightning,
Madly hurled through heaven and brightening
Voids of space, is our dread heightening ?

No ! we sneer ; oh God prolific !
If thou art immense, omnific,
Find some emblem more terrific

Than thy flame and detonation,
To o'erawe with grand probation
Men who scorn death's castigation !

Oh, Jehovah, glad or cheerless,
Armored in my doubt and tearless,
Unto thee I cry out, fearless !

If thou wishest I should render
Tribute to thy questioned splendor,
I, a worm and an offender,

From the sin that here betrays me,
From the depths of ennui raise me,
By the wings of white hope daze me !

If thou givest one poor token,
That the words thy Son hath spoken
By thee never shall be broken,

I exultant bells will ring thee,
And with loud voice I will sing thee
Psalms, and to high altars bring thee

Flowers and incense to adore thee,
In my mind as God restore thee,
And, repentant, bow before thee !

OMNIA POSSEDENS.

A Spirit Speaks.

Among the spirits of God's predilection
   I am and have been most supremely blest ;
   I am the one complete, the chosen and best,
The only one of absolute perfection !

Others, bewildered by the strength that bore them,
   Hold mighty tasks, yet humbly follow me
   As satellites their suns o'er land and sea,
But I, the vague and privileged, ignore them.

For the bold flower of my great elevation
   Bloomed from the chaos of incipient earth ;
   Before the stars my wonderment had birth ;
My power began at the sublime creation.

And, offspring of a grandeur all-transcending
   The subtle essence of all blight and stain,
   So long as air holds birds and fields give grain,
I shall exist and never know an ending.

God hath this much ordained by mandates glorious,
  And I, his slave, implicitly obey,
  While on dark, tireless wings from night to day
I soar, my mission to fulfill, victorious !

All that is feminine in Nature's beauty,
  All that conceives and bears I have possessed ;
  No more than restless waves have I known rest ;
Grand defloration is my gift, my duty !

In wondrous dreams, in ecstasies of slumber,
  All womankind has felt my thrill divine ;
  Virginities in trillions have been mine,
And countless ages can not name the number.

Sweet hosts of purity I have touched and tainted,
  And unto me for one brief span belonged
  Each thing productive that the world has thronged,
The hideous, vile and low, the fair, the sainted !

Receptively unconscious, every maiden
  . Born to this sphere beneath my kiss has bent,
  Yet unaware, in drowsiest content,
That by my fervor she was fed and laden.

Some wake at girlhood's passionate beginning,
  Filled with strange whims that make the dull flesh
      glad ;
  But they know not the blighting dream they had,
They can not fathom their celestial sinning.

No prayers or pleas have left them unmolested ;
  All once must feel my crude seraphic lust ;
  Omnipotence so wills, obey I must,
And, murmurless, obeying, have not rested.

And, since the awful advent of the ages,
  Before creative God his plans combined,
  In every atom-world my soul can find
The transient traces of its amorous rages !

Invisible, impalpable, erratic,
  I cull the bud of love upon each breast ;
  Red, holy lips are ravaged and caressed,
White forms are warmly held in bonds ecstatic.

And like a south breeze with sweet fragrance teeming,
  That robs a rose-core of its dawning charm
  So gently that it fosters no alarm,
I leave my sullied flesh-flowers calmly dreaming.

Each seed and plant that God on earth hath lavished
   I woo and win in infinite delight,
   And, in the solemn pauses of the night,
By me their modest redolence is ravished.

The distant suns, the stars serene and stainless,
   Atom and insect, fish, and brute, and bird,
   Alike are made submissive to my word
When'er I visit them in languor painless.

And in the spirit-seas of germs prolific,
   Domain of marvels veiled and blurred to man,
   Whose feeble sight their splendors can not span,
I roam unquestioned, worshiped, beatific !

For I lend life, like God, and my caresses,
   Discreetly foul, bring forth divine results ;
   Nativity in fearlessness exults ;
I am the spoiler that no thing oppresses !

Imposing shades and lights, that have existence
   Beyond the bounds of space, know life and love :
   I hold the vague virginities thereof ;
Unto my claims they offer no resistance !

And when I hear men cry in proud elation :
  "This woman I love is mine, and only mine !"
  My lips are curled in laughter saturnine,
For they know not my dominance and station.

Learn, oh ye rash and kiss-enraptured lovers,
  That she ye worship as a fleshy shrine,
  The loved one, rose-mouthed, plastic and divine,
Was mine and is ; my breath around her hovers.

Her beauteous body is my slave ; I use it.
  There is no secret in her burning form
  I have not mastered when with passion warm,
And she is repossessed when I so choose it.

Cleopatra in my bold embraces reveled ;
  Before lewd Faust I loved blonde Marguerite ;
  I bathed the brows of Beatrix the sweet,
My fire-kiss lingered in her hair disheveled.

All women who fill man's mind with admiration,
  The chosen of history that none forget,
  Semiramis, Virginia, Antoinette,
Helen and Ruth, were mine in fond prostration.

(9)

Naught sacred is exempted, for the Powers
    That gave me being haughtily ordained :
    "Go on thy way, and leave no thing unstained !
Sully the fruits, the blossoms and the flowers !"

And I, with jubilance complete and nameless,
    Obey the insolence of these commands,
    Speeding unwearied through unnumbered lands,
To soil all purities by men held blameless.

I choose the winning hour when beauty dreaming
    Awaits the coming lover with soft sighs,
    And I delight to note the half-closed eyes,
And all the mystic ardors gently teeming.

Morbid and mute, warm, fragrant and erotic,
    She lies in drowsy trances of desire ;
    Then I, to quench her ample bosom's fire,
Appear, appease, allay, in all despotic !

The sad and cloistered nun, who strives to sever
    The bonds of love and all that makes life fair,
    Whose pallid lips are ever parched by prayer,
In spite of missal and psalm is mine forever.

And when the heats of fancy brand and burn me,
  No modern Messalina, silk-arrayed,
  By haughty nonchalances can evade
The fury of my vast desires, or spurn me.

For I have portion in all things created ;
  My fecund breath has vivified dead spheres ;
  Yet, ah ! through wild eternities of years
I wander still, unsatisfied, unsated !

Men praise me unaware, and many a nation
  Bows low before the holy name of one
  I sent to save, adoring thus my son,
Christ, born of me, the world's supposed salvation.

And as years pass in fructuous progression,
  My labors, all incessant, thrive and grow,
  And I, whose empire none can overthrow,
Yearn more and more for limitless possession.

For often, alas ! when other loves have sued me,
  Fair virgins die, immaculately free,
  Buried in clay or in the moaning sea,
And, countenanced by Death, escape, elude me.

Then I, the germ-god, puissant and imperious,
   Must fly to rend the stillness of their tombs,
   And in the sepulchers' phantasmal glooms
Regain my ravished rights in ways mysterious.

*   *   *   *   *   *

Yet I, the lord of all, cry out in anger ;
   One being hath life I can not call my own,
   One miracle, one essence, one alone,
One that I crave for in delirious languor.

In her the roots of all things fair are blended ;
   She deigns to be, impeccable, sublime ;
   And since God murmured, "Let there now be time,"
She has existed, procreant and splendid.

And I, oh shame ! I, who should be partaker,
   Feel that her form I never shall possess ;
   For she in all her infinite stateliness
Is loved by God, my master and my maker !

LAZARUS.

I dwelt in sunny Bethany contented,
  Master of fertile lands and orchards rare,
  Housed with my sister Mary, who was fair,
  And Martha, who revered me as a prayer,
While naught the peace of my calm mind tormented.

The golden bees among my hives were many,
  My flowers and fruit were paid in Roman gold;
  The cattle and sleek sheep within my fold
  Were sought from distant Carmel to be sold,
And of annoying care I had not any.

Honored by all, and free from moods of sadness,
  I spent in courteous trade my pleasant days,
  With bond companions in delightful ways,
  And, like a bird loved by the jocund rays
Of happy spring, I passed the days in gladness.

Ah! I was blest indeed, for then the stately
    And gentle form of Christ did grace the land!
    Christ, who could heal and solace with his hand,
    Christ, the benign, the marvelous, the bland,
Who claimed me as his friend and loved me greatly.

And he in winning, simple ways had told me
    That I and all my house were joys to him,
    That he would gratify my every whim,
    And, that until my earthly eyes grew dim,
He would sustain, and strengthen, and uphold me.

His love, made manifest by proofs diurnal,
    Each hour more fervent and enduring seemed,
    And I, confiding in all wonders, deemed
    That he whose light celestial on me beamed
Would grant me life delicious and eternal.

And knowing it, glad, I smiled at mournful morrows,
    Childishly trusting in his word and might,
    And as I prayed below the stars at night,
    I felt he loved me, and in deep delight
I warned away the phantoms of all sorrows.

But on a day malarious ills came o'er me,
   While Christ, my holy friend, was wandering far,
   Preaching where green Judea's hillsides are ;
   Ay, far from *me* as earth is from a star,
And I no longer saw his smile before me.

Sharp throes and torrid harbingers of fever
   Came swift upon me, and I felt death nigh,
   And yet no tear regretful blurred my eye.
   Death will be balked ; *He* will not let me die,
He, the all-healing and sublime reliever.

Thus in my woe I raved, in anguish sighing,
   Tortured and bent, the prey to growing pain.
   My sisters sent quick messengers in vain,
   While he, who cleansed the lepers of the plain,
Abandoned me disconsolate and dying !

Ah ! cruelly he delayed and let me languish
   In those disastrous hours, undone and numb,
   Deaf to my cries and to my suffering dumb ;
   Yet, had he chosen in majesty to come,
I never would have known my present anguish.

     *   *   *   *   *   *

Then slowly I felt all sense and motion leave me ;
　　I knew no more of earth, for I had died
　　Among the loved ones sobbing by my side,
　　And, when a day in pallor I did abide,
The distant vault was opened to receive me.

Three days I lay a corpse in death's foul keeping,
　　Wrapped in dull cerements, hidden from all eyes,
　　Mourned by fond Mary, being then the prize
　　Of worms sepulchral, nevermore to rise,
While Mary swooned before the portal weeping.

And Jesus, who, when I was dead, had wandered,
　　Serenely preaching through Samaria's bloom,
　　Heedless of me and his impendent doom,
　　At last with weary feet approached my tomb,
And, seeing it closed, wept bitterly and pondered.

Then in a prayer supreme his strength assembling,
　　Raising unto the skies his holy head,
　　With hesitations all divine, he said :
　　"Come forth, oh Lazarus !" and from the dead
I rose, forthcoming, stupefied and trembling.

My eyes were blinded and my footsteps blundered,
  As he came toward me with a helping palm ;
  He touched me lightly, and his touch was balm,
  Giving to body strength, to spirit calm,
While the awed throng around him prayed and wondered !

When words were mine, I, then, the Heaven-protected,
  Eagerly bent my brows and whispered low :
  "Oh peerless friend !   Oh Christ who lov'st me so !
  Speak, shall I ever again death's odium know,
Now that by thee I have been resurrected ?"

And he, as if his miracle repenting,
  Cast down vague eyes and sadly murmured : "Yes !"
  Then turned away his face in deep distress,
  While I, dumbfounded and all wretchedness,
Spake no word more, but went my way lamenting.

* * * * * *

Gone was the dream magnificent I cherished
  For one brief span, and dulled was the sublime
  And senseless thought (perchance akin to crime)
  That by his will I could exist all time,
While *He* upon the cross was doomed to perish.

Ah ! Death in fearless ways makes no selection,
  Alike are slain the reptile and the bird ;
  No power its arm has haughtily deferred,
  And even the will of God is barely heard
By Death, the iconoclast of resurrection.

Now I pass on alone in grief religious,
  Once having changed the universal law,
  While men gaze on me in bewildered awe,
  As one who saw that which none other saw,
As one who knows God's mysteries prodigious.

I wander desolate, shunning friendly faces ;
  I fill the halls at night with hollow cries ;
  I see each morn the mocking red sun rise,
  That warns me one more day has come ; mine eyes
Are white with weeping in all lonely places.

A shadow of man, inconsequent and aimless,
  I keep my mighty secret unrevealed
  To man, but I have told it to the field,
  The trees, the stars, the stones, which will not yield
Its horror up, or tell its essence nameless.

Ah, Christ ! if thou art watching o'er me haggard,
   Pity and spare me through the coming years ;
   Compassion find for my incessant fears ;
   Remember thy past friendship and thy tears ;
Bid Death the second time be dull and laggard.

Ah, madman that I am ! Thou *canst* not save me !
   For I know *all*, Christ ! Thou hast not the power
   To stay the simple wilting of a flower,
   Or give unto the utter doomed an hour!
Death, death alone is great, and he can brave me !

Ah why, my Savior, didst thou strangely take me
   From dire annihilation's utter rest,
   Urged by my sister's sorrowing request ?
   Why, when the napkin on my brow was pressed,
Didst thou remove it, only to forsake me ?

Ah ! Death is sweeter than these living terrors,
   Haunted by hopelessness. I move afraid !
   Why for such torment was my spirit made ?
   Why, oh Redeemer, having greatly prayed,
Didst thou commit for me such harrowing errors ?

I love life *now!*　　I loath to leave the splendor
　　Of birdful groves and plains beloved of flowers ;
　　I venerate the olive glades and bowers,
　　And the fair sight of ivy-girdled towers
Thrills me as would a woman's accents tender.

I love the languors of the land Judean,
　　I love the sky when clouds or tempests pass,
　　I love the tangled emerald of its grass,
　　And all that moves or breathes therein.　　Alas !
I now must die again, oh Galilean !

I love to see all nature warm and glorious
　　Glow in the fecund pomp of autumn sheaves,
　　Fair in her redolent robes of rustling leaves,
　　Nature, that ever blossoms and conceives,
Life over death, exultant and victorious.

Ah ! if all things in mystic ways could borrow
　　The secret I have sternly kept, the trees
　　Would swoon and wither, and the weary breeze
　　Would die despondent, and caressing seas
Would lave sad shores no longer in their sorrow.

Each man on earth would shrink in consternation,
  Death would be feared, and God less loved than now ;
  No head would in Jehovan temples bow ;
  Men would respect no faith, no creed, no vow,
When having heard my mighty revelation !

For I, called Lazarus, the Resurrected,
  Affirm that false is what the Prophet saith ;
  I, who have seen decay, and doom, and death,
  Loudly attest, until my dying breath,
That we, earth's worms, by God are unprotected.

Beyond the tomb's *most explicable* portal,
  Shuddering, I tell to you that there is naught !
  Unteach, unteach, all that ye have been taught,
  Seek not, oh world ! what ye have ever sought !
There is no Heaven !   There is no soul immortal !

Hearken to me, oh multitudes ill-fated,
  Ye who through life so penitently plod,
  Bending before a phantom creed and rod,
  Know there is no hereafter and no God,
Know that your every hope will be frustrated.

For life beyond the tomb existed never.
   Nothingness, void and silence come to all.
   Pray not, for none will ever hear your call ;
   Pray not, for Death's chill answer will appall ;
The soul dies with the body and forever.

There is no fertile Paradise that waits us
   When flesh doth rot, and what we call a soul
   Is matter, like our flesh, and hath no goal ;
   No pitying angels with our pains condole ;
There is no hope when cruel death prostrates us.

I have been dead ; the sepulcher did take me ;
   Yet I knew naught, although they do assert
   I lay for days in dolorous gloom inert ;
   Yet to naught palpable can I revert,
Till the calm voice of Jesus did awake me.

No dream, no vision lulled me as I rested,
   No sight celestial did I see, no sound
   Of angel songs did in my ears resound ;
   No sense, no thought came to me prone and bound,
Until his word my deathliness molested.

Yet for three days I lay in dismal cerements,
   Three days and nights, while no thing did I see ;
   Oh ! hesitant friend, why didst thou come to me,
   Bid Death depart, command me to be free,
And honor me there with thy serene endearments ?

For *nothing, nothing* lasts ; the world is dreaming
   Of future joys that earthly bliss transcend ;
   When dead, I say, our souls with nothing blend.
   Death is the sad, inevitable end,
And after, there is hope not, nor redeeming.

And that is why I love in vales Judean
   To wander, drinking life at every pore,
   Praising the sea and worshiping the shore,
   For I shall once more die and hear no more
The voice of spring-time and the linnet's pæan.

And that is why I linger in the gladness
   Of town and village, mountain-way and plain,
   Moved. even in my unutterable pain,
   With love for all I shall not see again,
Filled with perpetual and persistent sadness.

April 23, 1879.

BABEL.

In ways unknown to mortals, I regret
  The memory of that grand and haughty hour
  When the symmetric splendor of my tower
Awed the pale Heaven, that braves my anger yet.

No stone of mine, now crumbling, can forget
  My palm-clad pomp in those great days of power,
  When my colossal summit made stars cower
And shrink before my rising silhouette.

Oh ! despicable, puny hordes of men !
  When I held sky and space within my reach,
What souls had ye to be thus overcome ?
Why did your coward hands desert me when
  Jehovah in his wrath had blent all speech ?
Could ye not work, oh fools ! though ye were dumb ?

1878.

CARTHAGE.

CARTHAGE.

SONG OF NEGRO SLAVES.

We were trapped in far oases,
And the darkness of our faces
Proclaims that for hard slavery and trouble we were born,
To live here as thralls and wretches,
With the beasts, on herbs and vetches,
The poor toilers of the city, the proud Carthaginian's scorn.

In our land of moss and melons
We lived not as hated felons;
We were princes plumed and radiant and the lords of many
    herds.
And we loved our shining beaches
And the fertile forest-reaches,
Ay ! we loved the whir of arrows and the melodies of birds.

We had many a dusky maiden,
With white shells and coral laden,
To admire our agile dances and to give us kisses sweet ;

We had countless flocks and shepherds,
And the glossy skins of leopards
Made us mantles for our bodies and soft covers for our feet.

We had captured skulls, as rightful,
In our tented towns delightful,
Ay ! the skulls of those we hated and in loyal combat killed ;
For our race was ever glorious
And eternally victorious,
While the rustle of our lances every soul with terror filled.

But there came a time of terror,
A sad day of wrong and error,
When the cavalry of Carthage, we had never met before,
By new modes and ways of battle
Mowed us down like helpless cattle,
And our king was left beheaded while the jackals drank his gore.

So, bereft of love, we languish
In our misery and anguish,
By our mighty gods forsaken while our brothers mourn our loss ;
And we wait, bowed down in sorrow,
For the dire and dreaded morrow,
When to please the conquering rabble we shall writhe upon
the cross !

SONG OF CARTHAGINIAN SAILORS.

We are monarchs of the sea,
And before us ever flee
The great vessels of the Romans, ay, like doves before the
thunder !
We can terrify all Rome,
When we speed through blood and foam
To their harbors and their vineyards, there to revel and to
plunder !

We can count ten thousand oars
Upon our and distant shores,
On our haughty prows e'er glitter the fierce eyes of sculptured
horses ;
We are dreaded as a pest
By our enemies oppressed,
And the beaches of their inlets are all crimson with their corses.

Oh ! we long to sail again
To the fair Sicilian main,
For great Melcarth is propitious, and the skies are full of omens.

And with fury we will fall
On the coasts and slaughter all
The effeminate and craven haughty rabble of the Romans !

Yea ! we clamor for the fray ;
We have spent our spoil and pay,
And we need the touch of money and the clinking of rare prizes,
While a hatred of the foe
Makes our martial bosoms glow,
And our cry for blood and battle in magnificence arises !

In mean leather coin they pay
Our great services to-day,
For the Senate dreams or revels and forgets its staunch
    defender !
We need purple gold and bright,
And more women for the night,
Ay ! more women, white and wanton, women oiled, and sweet,
    and tender.

Where is Hanno with his sword ?
Our great admiral and lord
Must be hot with wine and spices in the chambers of a harlot,

For he hath deserted now
His victorious vessel's prow,
And doth chant the praise of Tanit in his rustling robes of
    scarlet.

Are we doomed no more to fight
And to burn great towns at night ?
Must we linger here like fish-men, gazing calmly at the water ?
Oh, great Hanno ! rise ! appear !
Beckon Romeward with thy spear,
For we yearn to hear the trumpets drown the shrieking and the
    slaughter.

CRUCIFIXION OF A CARTHAGINIAN GENERAL.

And lo ! Adherbal, General-in-Chief,
The leader of the Slingers of the Isles,
Captain of Cohorts and Iberian slaves,
Captain of Libyan and Phœnician spears,
Captain of Greeks, Campanians and Gauls,
And many Volscians, famed for battle-cries,
Had lost a contest on Sicilian plains,
Leaving a thousand warriors dead or maimed,
And twenty elephants, the dread of Rome.
Yea, and his foolish plans had cost the State
A hundred tents of silk and many spears,
And bales of food and money for the troops
In two besiegéd towns, and camels, too,
While all the jeweled women of the camp,
Marching to render pleasure to the men,
Had fallen captives to the power of Rome,
To be the playthings of centurions.

And Carthage shook with anger, and the gods
Howled from their altars in terrific wrath,

Claiming the sacrifice of Adherbal,
Whom they forsook as ravens shun dry bones.
And all the people clamored to the gods.
And lo ! the sapient council filled the streets
And halls judicial near the shrine of Bel,
There with unhallowed speed to judge the cause,
Dooming the vanquished general to the cross.

And he, Adherbal, paled before the speech,
But murmured not, because his soul was brave.
And as he sinned by sleeping with his slaves,
White Gallic women captured on the hills,
When over plans he should have worn his eyes,
He merited the doom, and courted it.
While people praised his valor near to death,
And crowded near to hear his dying wish,
Which would be granted him by antique law,
If that he begged not life ; and Adherbal
Arose, with sensuous smiles upon his lips
And passionate gleams of fire within his eyes,
And cried aloud : " Honored and holy law !
I will abide by thee and have no fear.
The boon thou grantest, ere my days are snapped
Asunder like a rotten reed, is this :
Grant me the secrecy of purple tents,

Bring me Campanian wine with meat and figs,
And until dawn leave me in guarded peace
With yonder lustrous maiden of the Gauls,
Whom I with mine own hand in battle seized
When she had pierced my leathers with a dart
And conquered me.   I there, her conqueror,
Let me but hide the bristles of my beard
Upon the rounded whiteness of her breasts,
And at the hour appointed I will die,
Loving the law and faithful to the land !"
And all the people shouted :   "Grant the wish !"
And it was granted.

                  Through the balmy night
The fallen chief made revel with the maid,
And bade her note his valor on the cross.
And when the dawn, with its sweet pulse of light,
Had throbbed through darkness to a perfect day,
He was led forth and nailed unto a cross.
Now, in the horde that compassed him about,
Was an old warrior, who had warred in Spain
When young Adherbal first sniffed blood on fields,
And in the panic of a battle's heart
He, crushed and trampled on by yelling hosts,
Lay stricken down and was about to die,

When lo ! Adherbal, witnessing his plight,
Charged on the assailers, and with mighty blows
Saved the poor man and vanquished on that day.
And the old soldier's mind was full of this.
He saw again the swift, tumultuous scene
Pass in his eyes, and there his savior hung,
Nailed to a cross to linger in the sun,
The prey of birds, and all his soul rebelled.
And when the throngs were busy at the sight,
He crouched and poised a javelin in his hand,
And with unerring speed above the heads
Of all the multitude it shrilly whirred
Deep to the tortued bosom of the chief,
Who cried aloud : " Bel bless thee, friend ! " and died,
While all the cheated people turned in wrath
And tore the soldier's body into shreds.

CARTHAGINIAN MARKET SONG.

Oh sweet passer, pause, be wise !
We have flowers to charm thine eyes.
Enter, passer, stop, sweet stranger, enter in and taste
    our wares !
We have rosy auroch-flesh
From the green oases fresh,
We have melons from Egesta and the juicy Sulci pears.

In our baskets thou wilt find
Hottest spice of every kind,
With rich paste to rub the body when the sun is fierce
    by day.
They are delicate and sweet,
Made of myrrh, and wine, and wheat,
Ay! with sulphur, and pure galbanum, and the milk of
    bitches gray.

We have fat and sweetened moles,
And rich safran in clay bowls ;
We have locusts fried and crackling with a savor of the
    palms ;

We have lobsters and small fish
To prepare a dainty dish,
And young dogs, made sleek with olives, stuffed with
    annis-bread and balms.

Taste our cool Campanian wine,
Fit for any god divine !
Taste our figs from Agrigentum and our shell-fish from
    Hagour.
From Selimis we have snails
Breathing still among the pails,
And we catch the thorny porcupine in ravine and on
    moor.

We have garum, and at noon
We have cakes shaped like the moon,
With young camel's flesh in plenty and the luscious
    hearts of deer ;
We sell plates of peacock's brains,
And the mighty narwhale canes,
Yea, and perfumed bags to shelter soldiers' beards when
    rains appear.

Oh sweet passer, pause and choose !
We have ornamented shoes

Made from skins of striped hyenas caught by hunters
in their home.
And our prices, passer fair,
Ay, our prices, passer rare,
Are far cheaper, yea, far cheaper than the prices of foul
Rome !

SONG OF ROMAN PRISONERS.

In the scorching sun amid the bricks we languish,
  And no golden ransom cometh o'er the foam ;
We are slaves in utter misery and anguish,
  Left unshielded by the generals of Rome.

We are doomed by mighty beasts to be down-trampled,
  Or upon a hideous cross to shriek and rot,
If to save us for our valor unexampled
  Our companions from the Forum hurry not.

We were captured in the fierce heart of the battle,
  But no warrior brought a pallor to our cheeks ;
We withstood the many darts that smite and rattle,
  We were terrorized by no Numidian shrieks.

But our blood forsook us when those beasts Titanic,
  Those ponderous monsters, trod our legions down,
And our gods deserted us in hideous panic,
  While we battled for our citadel's renown !

When the sacred band of Mégara assaulted
   Our unbroken lines with many a savage cry,
We defied their power and all their gods exalted,
   And like heroes we were jubilant to die !

But we war not with strange monsters and with devils,
   To the gleam of tusks we dare not trust our eyes,
When a fierce and snorting brute in armor levels
   Half a legion to the dust before it dies !

Man to man in equal battle we fight gravely ;
   Lance to lance, and sword to sword, we know no fears ;
We repel attack and urge our chargers bravely
   Through a maze of shields and labyrinths of spears !

Oh great Rome ! Oh mother-city ! strike, and spare us
   From ignoble death upon these arid sands !
To thy walls impregnable in triumph bear us,
   Place our captured glaives once more within our hands !

CHORUS OF PRIESTS.

Oh mighty Moloch !   Hail, terrific god, bull-headed !
And hail to thee, Râháb, omnipotent and dreaded !
Baal-Sâmín, unto thee, God of Celestial Spaces,
We come with precious gifts and pallor on our faces !
And, at thy shrine, Zeboub, great God of Rot and Carrion,
We offer piles of human flesh and praise thee with the clarion !
God of the Holy Hills, strong Peor, we adore thee,
And in our pointed caps we humbly bow before thee !
Dercéto, unto thee, sweet goddess finned and beauteous,
We come with gems and gifts, thy people grave and duteous !
And to thy sacred shrine, oh Nebo ! black and awful,
We drag the shrieking slaves for sacrifices lawful ;
We smear thy statue's brass with rarest spice and butter,
While at its polished base thy gory victims mutter !
We hail thee, Mastimán, God of the Dead and Dying !
Before thy shrine of gold still kneel the doomed ones sighing !
And unto thee, Gurzíl, we bring fat, dreamy cattle,
And redden with their veins thy grees, oh God of Battle !

(11)

In fires of Sandarác we burn black cocks and chickens,
While in the pots the seething spice in clouds of fragrance
    thickens.
Protect your slaves, oh mighty God ! and let us languish never,
So that we may in swoóns of joy bow down to thee forever !

CHORUS OF CARTHAGINIAN SOLDIERS.

Every foe before us flies

With a terror in his eyes !

We are Hannibal's fierce warriors for all battle-carnage frantic,

And amid our brazen shields,

In the blood of many fields,

He, our leader, our great Captain, deigns to praise our deeds

gigantic !

On the slopes of Eryx far

We did mutilate and mar

The mailed enemies who scorned us with mad folly and

derision !

How Zeboub, the God of Rot,

Who his chosen ne'er forgot,

Hurled his lightning on their bodies as they vanished like a

vision !

Yea ! Zeboub doth love us well !

In his name we smite and fell

Without grace and without mercy all the vanquished of each

city !

We are deaf to captive's cries,

We are stone to woman's sighs,

For great Melcarth guides us onward and hath never taught

us pity!

With the fat a foe-corpse yields

We illuminate our shields,

Made of brass and hides of elephants, whose strength defies

all arrows ;

And we feast with joys immense

In our white and purple tents,

In the glory of our manhood, in the splendor of our marrows !

When we valorously march

Over plain and under arch,

We have with us dogs and leopards, and lithe lynxes, pets

ferocious,

And when blood is thick and red,

To the carrion they are led,

And the wounded foeman shiver in their massive jaws

atrocious !

We have taken scores of towns,

On the hills and on the downs,

Ay ! Entella, Cirta, Tingis, and walled Henna towered and

flowerful !

We have made a dreaded camp
Under Cyrnos bleak and damp,
And have crushed the Roman legions under chariots swift
and powerful!

Great Xantippus, once our Chief,
Who in battle knew no grief,
Led us forward when at Adis all our enemies assembled ;
Ask the devasting crows,
That devoured the fallen rows,
How they found annihilation while their coward Senate
trembled !

We parade in brazen bands,
We have jewels on our hands,
Our campaigns are ever counted by the rings upon our fingers ;
And whenever we appear,
The stupendous God of Fear
On the forehead of the Romans in a mist of scarlet lingers !

We have bridles of bent reeds
To direct our bounding steeds ;
They are burdened by the bodies of the Roman girls we
capture,

Ay ! the blushing Roman girls,
With a fragrance in their curls,
Whom we kiss and fondle nightly, warm with rosy wine and
 rapture !

We perpetually burn
For a kiss's soft return,
And when noble War has ended to the Satheb we can wander,
 Where the city harlots stride
 In their jewels and their pride,
Where we bend upon their bosoms and the Roman silver
 squander !

Oh great Gurzíl, God of War,
Mighty God without a scar !
Drive the enemies of Carthage now before thee like dumb
 cattle,
 And with fury in thine eyes,
 Deign impeccable to rise,
And protect our valiant foreheads in the hot hells of the battle !

WAR SONG OF NUMIDIAN HORSEMEN.

We are the terror of the state,
    And yet its joy ;
Our blows are pitiless as fate
    When we destroy.

We are the mighty army's heart ;
    Our glittering shields,
When seen, make haughty Romans start
    On battle-fields.

Unhampered course our valiant steeds
    On plain and shore,
Held by a wreath of twisted reeds
    And nothing more.

Our ears are gemmed with ocean pearls ;
    We are revered,
And we have perfume in our curls
    And on our beard.

Agile and fearless everywhere,
    The foe we meet,
Dealing forth danger and despair,
    Death and defeat.

A thousand Romans by our spears
    Have lost their lives,
And in our camp, with wine that cheers,
    We hold their wives.

The vestals and the maids of Rome
    Our couch adorn ;
Our gaudy tents become their home
    From dusk to morn.

The courtesans of Malqua come
    To sell delight ;
With spicy food and birds that hum
    We pass the night.

Without us, Carthage in despair
    Would surely fall ;
The banners of the state we bear
    . High over all.

The strength of great Melcarth is ours.
  Stronger than brass !
Bow to the dust, and strew with flowers
  The path we pass !

SONG OF NECROMANCERS.

The secrets we divine
Of stars that o'er us shine,
And Tanit, bathed in splendors,
Her mystery surrenders
    At our sign.

Each living thing on earth
Proclaims our holy worth ;
We know all wonders mystic,
All symbols cabalistic,
    From our birth.

We know the balm for stings,
We read the eyes of kings ;
We live in contemplation,
And in deep meditation
    Learn all things.

We warn when gentle rain
Will ripple on the plain.
Near Nebo's lofty altars
Our worship never falters,
Nor is vain.

We read the azure skies,
All naked to our eyes !
And nothing over or under
Can cause our spirit wonder
Or surprise !

We know the mystic powers
Of birds, and beasts, and flowers ;
And happy life eternal,
Forever sweet and vernal,
Will be ours !

CRUCIFIXION OF LIONS.

And lo! the pale announcer of new moons,
High on the flowerful Temple of Eschmôn,
Cried to the winds and smote his palsied cheek.
For he was feverish by the midnight air
Of many decades, and his blood was thin
Attending to the motions of the orb
That turned his eyes to whiteness, but he knew
That, when fell blindness shrouded them at last,
He would be sacred held, and he was glad
Within his bosom, for the moon's thin slaves,
When ravaged by the splendor of her rays,
Were holy ever after, and could dwell
In Mégara, the suburb of the town,
Under green palms and fountains, with the birds,
There to praise Melcarth in the glorious sun,
And feast on fat, and know the taste of quails,
Or drain Campanian amphoras at night.
Therefore, Maharbal on the temple's crown
Signaled a wondrous darkness on the moon,
That presaged death to animals that night,

And on his silver trumpet he announced
The serious changes in the heavens afar.

His words, caught up by sentries at the gates,
Were hurried to a myriad of ears,
And Schahabarim, the anointed priest,
Paused in the act of sacrifice, and bade
A thousand slaves to hasten to the pits,
And shackle thirty lions with strong gyves.

And this was done amid a storm of roars
And death to many by colossal fangs ;
For twenty men sufficed to bind a beast :
Yea, twenty only !   When the beast was bound,
Two, sometimes three, of the lithe negro slaves
Lived to narrate the combat to the town !
And as the sacred number, thirty, stood,
Full half a thousand human lives were lost.
But loss of life it was not, they being slaves
Unworthy to drag offal to old bears.
Then all the people shouted at the groans
Of bleeding wretches, and the living slaves,
Tottering from effort and terrific wounds,
With strips of skin still dangling on their loins,
With opened shoulders bitten to the bone,

Led forth the monsters to the neighboring grove,
Where Tanit shone in miracles of light.

Here were a hundred crosses black with blood
Of man and beast, the victims of the month.
Some were alive and howled aloud for death,
And some were dead, and others had no eyes,
But breathed amid the rustling wings of birds,
Half frenzied by the approach of golden light,
Loath to abandon many a half-picked bone,
Glossy through clots of blood below the moon.
And many crosses held no putrid weight,
But skeletons of prisoners of war
Who paid no ransom, and these bones were torn
Free from the rusty nails and hurled away,
To give a place for all the lions there.
Ay, with such savage force, such eager haste,
That many a rotting palm or foot remained
And stunk upon the cross, the body gone !

Then the high priests of Moloch oiled and robed,
With ringéd finger and large ebon lyres,
Advanced and stood before the crosses grim,
Singing their holy souls forth to the moon.

Then with a rush, a tumult and great cries,
The thousand slaves fell on the shackled beasts
And nailed their writhing limbs upon the cross,
Biting their brows and tearing out their manes,
While angry teeth snapped loudly in their arms,
And yells excruciating moved the gods.
For many hours in bloody sweat and fear
They fought the monsters maddened by the light,
And when the last was firm upon the cross,
Slaves there were few to taunt the vanquished foe.
The lions roared in agony of pain,
And clamoring echoed to the halls of Bel,
Filling the hearts of worshipers with bliss,
And as they roared, the people, red with joy,
Seized the bright flaring torches all about
To singe their open jaws, their shattered limbs,
And hail their gods and thank them for the sport.
But, as they trifled in this way, the hours
Passed slowly on, and from the temple's heights,
A chant proclaimed the pleasure of the gods,
And that white Tanit's heart was satisfied.
Therefore, the people hurried to the town
And left the groaning lions to the moon.

SONG TO TANIT.

CARTHAGINIAN SONG TO THE MOON.

Oh luminous Tanit! unto us thou sendest
  The wandering winds, the dews and many rains,
And by thy wondrous rise and fall thou lendest
  New mysteries to our green, abundant plains.

The eyes of cats grow narrow by thy changes,
  The spots of panthers by thy rays expand,
And fearless beasts within the mountain ranges
  Grow terrible or weak at thy command.

The shells that dot the tawny beach thou fillest,
  Thou makest pearls, pale jewels of the sea,
And with great awe our listening ears thou thrillest
  By all the grace that emanates from thee.

The corpses of our foes thou putrefiest,
  Thou callest phantoms and destructive dreams ;
Thou art our blessed Tanit, purest, highest !
  We worship in bewilderment thy beams !

Oh, thou art white, and luminous, and splendent !
  Thou art serene, immaculate, complete,
Pacing the skies with all thy stars attendant,
  And Carthage like a jewel at thy feet !

Thine eyes devour our temples and our altars,
  Thy sheen doth even sicken the sacred apes ;
Their bestial courage in thy presence falters,
  Their sense is terrorized by heavenly shapes.

Oh Tanit ! whitest moon, forever holy !
  Watch us and guard us from thy distant throne !
Thee will we venerate and worship solely,
  Thou of all goddesses art pure alone !

SONG OF HANNIBAL'S WARRIORS.

Hail, Hannibal! to thee
Belong the land and sea!
Before thee foemen flee
    Like frightened horses!
The legions of the State
Thy valor consecrate,
And ever victorious great
    Crown all our forces!

Thou art above all law,
Supreme and without flaw;
We follow thee with awe
    And passive wonder!
We reverence thy choice,
And in thy deeds rejoice;
The war-cry of thy voice
    Is like a thunder!

Oh Hannibal ! we crave
From thee a soldier's grave,
When with a dripping glaive
  We strike the foemen ;
And if we have to die,
Let our last battle-cry
Ascend to Bel on high
  O'er corses Roman !

The maidens of the foe
Are soft and warm, we know ;
We love the ruby glow
  Of their sweet blushes.
Oh Victor ! lead to Rome
Thy legions through the foam,
And give to us a home
  Near Roman rushes !

We long to smite and burn,
And childish pity spurn ;
For blaring camps we yearn,
  And deadly battle !

We long to make more slaves,
And dig great Roman graves,
Or hurl them to the waves
    Like sickened cattle !

Oh Hannibal ! arise
With vengeance in thine eyes !
Answer our battle-cries,
    So that thy glory,
Thy glory great and vast,
When we from earth have passed,
May for all ages last
    In song and story !

SONG OF THE WAŶ-WALKER.

Oh, listen, passer dear !
Behold me, I am here,
Deftly oiled, and lithe and supple, with red roses on my
breast.
Bid me to thee by a sign ;
Give me gold and I am thine,
For I long by valiant warriors to be petted and caressed !

I have amulets and rings,
And a host of peerless things
In my perfumed house in Malqua ; come, sweet passer, to my
home !
There are lilies in my hair,
And my bosom, round and bare,
Is far whiter than pale Tanit beaming softly on the foam.

I have spices and rich paint,
And my limbs are without taint ;
I will sing for thee and play thee merry tunes on tambourines.

I will dance to lend new fire
To the pangs of thy desire,
And will fill thy soul with cloyment 'mid the garlands of my
screens.

Lo! behold me in my pride!
For my rosy cheeks are dyed,
And my feet are cased in sandals all besprent by sparkling stones,
And within my pleasant house
For a night thou canst carouse,
Softly pleasured by the music of the flutes of asses' bones.

I have soothing paste and wine
From the scented lotus-vine,
I have marble baths and unguents to refresh the wearied frame ;
For the ravishments that swarm
In my body white and warm
Are as sweet as waving frondage and as subtle as a flame.

I can resurrect thy fire
By the thrumming of my lyre ;
In my nudity delicious I will make thy spirit sigh,
For all doleful sorrow slips
From the fragrance of my lips,
And all pains and sad vexations on my perfumed body die.

BEL-SHAR-UZZUR.

(*BELSHAZZAR.*)

A DRAMATIC POEM.

BEL-SHAR-UZZUR.

The lady of kingdoms.

—Jeremiah, 51: 41.

The praise of the whole earth.

—Isaiah, 47: 5.

Is not this great Babylon, that I have built for the house of the kingdom by the might of my power, and for the honor of my majesty?

—Daniel, 4: 30.

Belshazzar the king made a great feast to a thousand of his lords, and
drank wine before the thousand.

—Daniel, 5: 1.

They drank wine and praised the gods of gold and of silver, of brass, of
iron, of wood, and of stone.

—Daniel, 5: 4.

A mighty nation, an ancient nation.

—Jeremiah, 5: 15.

And he called the Chaldeans and said, whosoever shall read the writing
and show me the interpretation thereof shall be clothed with scarlet, and
have a chain of gold about his neck, and shall be the third ruler of the
kingdom.

I will punish Bel in Babylon, and I will bring out of his mouth that
which he hath swallowed up, and the nations shall not flow together any
more unto him ; yea, the walls of Babylon shall fall.

And Babylon, the glory of kingdoms, the beauty of the Chaldees'
excellency, shall be as when God overthrew Sodom and Gomorrah.

—Isaiah, 13: 19.

It shall never be inhabited, neither shall it be dwelt in from generation to generation, neither shall the Arabian pitch tent there, neither shall the shepherds make their fold there.

But wild beasts of the desert shall be there, and their houses shall be full of doleful creatures, and owls shall dwell there, and satyrs shall dance there.

And the wild beasts of the islands shall cry in their desolate houses, and dragons in their pleasant palaces ; and her time is near to come, and her days shall not be prolonged.

—Isaiah, 13: 19.

Sit thou silent and get thee into darkness, O daughter of the Chaldeans, for thou shalt no more be called the lady of the kingdoms.

—Isaiah, 47: 5.

Bel boweth down, Nebo stoopeth.

—Isaiah, 46: 1.

Babylon hath been a golden cup in the Lord's hand, that made all the earth druken ; the nations have drunken of her wine, therefore the nations are mad.

—Jeremiah, 51: 7.

Babylon is suddenly fallen and destroyed ; howl for her ; take balm for her pain, if so be she may be healed.

O thou that dwellest upon many waters, abundant in treasures, thine end is come, and the measure of thy covetousness.

And Bablyon shall become heaps, a dwelling place for dragons, an astonishment, and a hissing without an inhabitant.

—Jeremiah, 51: 37.

BEL-SHAR-UZZUR.

SCENE I.

BABYLON.—THE CITY.

The stainless sun arose and with warm rays
Bathed Babylon in fluttering waves of gold,
While through the fertile plains of palm and grain
The reedy Araxes like a snake of steel
Crawled, with its ripples breaking into blue.
Huge Imgur-Bel, the vast and inner wall
Made lustrous by the warriors' shining shields,
Thrust to the sky in overwhelming pride
Its haughty bastions peopled like a hive,
And, from the outer works, Nimetti-Bel,
The bearded guards looked down upon the roads,
Watching the loading of an hundred mules,
With neighing steeds, and camels gaunt, in lines
That reached unto Borsippa, for the time
For caravans had come, and from the town
Each day in stately numbers they went forth

To Bactria, Media and to Persia, where
They sold and bartered Babylonia's wealth.
Then oxen, panting by the wooden goad,
Passed slowly through the city's brazen gates,
With tearful eyes appealing to the slaves;
From Calah came they, laden with fresh figs
From Erech, Opis and Rehoboth too,
Dragging rich grain, and lettuce, and sweet fruit.
Ay, and from Sŭrripac, and from Nipŭr,
From Resen and Arbela, and Accad,
And from great Nineveh, the sister town.
Swift cedar-boats upon the Libil passed,
And, on the Naharmalcha, known to all
As the canal of great Bel-shar-uzzŭr,
Innumerable vessels steered by slaves
Were rowed with jests and curses to the marts.
The marts colossal of the mighty town,
Deep in its leafy heart of cedar groves,
Near Ai-ipur-sabu, the reservoir
That yielded water for the eager throats
Of sweating captives building in the sun.
From Sittacè they came, and from Ashur,
And from Sargina and Nitocris lake,
Reeking with heavy odors of hot spice

Sweet unto the fragrance of unnumbered flowers,
Burdened with melons and the dainty date.
Then in the booths and corners of the mart
The pleasant wares were garnered, and the crowds
With money in their palms walked to and fro,
Tasting and handling ere they purchase made,
And as they passed and sneered at perfect things
Made for their delectation by the gods,
The market women called to them and sang.

MARKET SONG.

Oh good passers, stop and buy ;
Lend an ear unto our cry ;
We have locusts parched and luscious, steeped and sweetened
    in sweet rain.
We have honey in clay jars,
White and golden as the stars,
And fat Phasion quails in saffron pierced and captured on
    the plain.

We have cinnamon and myrrh,
And the mountain foxes' fur,
We have spikenard, and red resin, and sweet incense at your
    choice ;
We have bdellium, spice and salt,
And e'en Beetis would exalt
All our oils, and leeks, and perfumes, that can make the heart
    rejoice.

From Sippara and Ashur,
And from redolent Nipur,
We buy melons, kids and cassia, and the sweet surripac milk ;

And from Nineveh the grand
We have brought with our own hand
Choicest flour and fruit, and natron, and the sacred violet silk,

We have pretty birds that hum,
We have barley-bread and gum,
We have snouts of boars and badgers and the tender flanks of
    deer ;
From Kutu we led with pains
Many mules with many grains ;
We have Eshcol wine in plenty and ripe figs from Calat near.

We sell dewy plants and flowers
To make sweet the sultry hours ;
We have herbs that heal diseases, and the oil of the tamar;
We have venoms, drugs and balms,
And the frondage of the palms,
And the produce of great Egypt brought o'er deserts from
    afar.

Ah, good passer, pause and buy ;
Lend an ear unto our cry ;
For the gods and for your dwellings, for the beggar, for the
    beast,

You can find of every kind,
To suit fancy, taste and mind,
For the altars of the temple or the splendor of the feast.

We have clover sweet and fresh
To adorn the young lamb's flesh;
We have lettuce, grapes and madder, and the dainty durra-
maise ;
We have olives fat or sour,
And new lemons packed in flour,
With rare apricots and peaches culled on green Accadian ways.

Then would the wealthy purchase half a booth,
And the thin poor would stealthily approach
And give their last small earning for a leek.

THE PALACE.

And in the square arose the king's great home,
The palace of the Lord Bel-shar-uzzur,
A miracle, a wonder, a delight,
Guarded by forms majestic, and the brows
Of puissant gods, and bulls with human heads,
Wingéd like eagles, aye, and figures strange,
Erect or couchant, monsters carved in stone,
In gold, in iron, in agate and in wood,
Emblems sublime, a tribute to the gods !
Lo ! there were many carvings on the walls
In high relief, with clarity of tints ;
Memorials of the triumphs of the kings
Here were set forth so that all eyes might see
The rare presentment of the chase's joys,
And all the stern vicissitudes of war ;
And, in artistic chaos, on all sides
Were figures of grim horsemen, bulls and boars,
With wounded lions and fleet-footed stags
Running by rivers, towns and arméd towers,
And with them there were chariots and slaves,
And many forms that strangers marveled at.

Above a hundred stately pillars rose,
Supporting painted chambers firmly roofed
With polished cedars crusted o'er with gold,
Daubed with vermilion to assault the eye ;
And still above these lofty rooms there stood
One other, built on ivory columns, carved
In rarest ways, beneath a roof of gold ;
While, above all, a miracle of skill,
Was poised the ever-sacred pure retreat
Destined and held for King Bel-shar-uzzur,
When to the stately gods he deigned to pray.

Firm by the palace gate stood two great pillars
Of rarest sardonyx, to make innocuous
All deadly drugs, all deleterious poisons,
And the vast breathing body of the palace
Was held by glittering columns in such numbers
As were the days within the year Assyrian,
Or furlongs in the circuit of the city.

Then came a cry, and lo ! with avid eyes
The people rushed into the temple's court,
For one, a bearded Jew, had spat, and spat,
Nine times upon the marble of a god !

And he was bruised and beaten by the crowd,
And there was blood upon his breast and hair,
For children in their spite had torn it forth.
And they were right, for all the people laughed,
And showed him limpid water in a bowl,
For well they knew he thirsted and was faint,
And then they spilled it on the passing swine.

He cried unto Jehovah, and his God
Was silent as a grain of sun-cursed sand,
And then the people laughed again and pierced
His filthy flanks with bodkins, for the Jew
Was lean and bony, and his only food
Was garbage thrown as offal from the walls,
By the Araxes to be carried far.
"Good God, Jehovah, pity him!" they cried.

Then from the temple came two beardless slaves,
And drave into the earth a rod of brass,
And caught the Jew as would a child a toy,
Then, poising him with hideous jests, they forced
His quivering body down upon the point
And left him groaning, calling to his God.

And then the people danced with all delight,
Smiting the Jew with stones and rotten fruit,
Aping his groans and writhing, as they cried :
"Call to thy Jew-God !   Bid him save thee now !"
And he said naught, while the trained slaves drew near,
And by his sweating head they pushed him down
Further and further on the glittering rod,
That shone like gold upon the setting sun.

One groan he made, one long and piteous groan,
Then strove to twist his body in such way
That the offending brass would pierce the heart,
For well he knew that if he failed in this,
For hours, even days, he would live hopeless there,
With water none, the target of the town.

And he did fail, and all the people knew
That he had failed, and yelled a mad applause,
For now he had no strength to give the twist.
"Sweet Jew!" they cried, "watch now the temple's birds;
They love thee and are fond of Jewish meat.
Dung for their taste !"   And as they spake, the crows
And carrion-kites of Babylonia swept

Above his yellowing skin and made the air
Dizzy with ebon tumult, ere they swooped
With fearful hookéd claws upon their prey,
And plucked his arid eyes out for their food.

Again the people shouted, and the Jew,
Sightless and livid, murmured to his God,
And he was heard.   A tremor shook his bones,
And he was dead.   And then the crowd grew still,
Whispering to one another in dismay :
" *Who is the God Jehovah he adores ?* "

SCENE II.

Above the splendor of the brazen gates,
Above the walls of hieroglyphic brick,
Where three war-chariots manned could run abreast,
Above the parapets of inlaid gold,
Above the porticoes with cedar beamed,
Above the arches, terraces and all
The matchless masonry of the regal town,
Arose the hanging gardens, blessed with birds
And many jutting fountains, and great oaks,
Ay, musical at eve with moaning palms ;

For they were fashioned in this wise to cheer
Nebuchadnezzar's ever holy wife,
Sweet Amyitis, who was mountain-born,
Far on the Empire's borders, and she yearned
For leagues of grass and shadows of great trees.
And Babylon, the queen of arts and arms,
Of mirth and warfare, and all glorious things,
Was unto her a monster girt in brass,
Cursed by a stinging sun, a thing to hate.
Therefore the grandsire of Bel-shar-uzzur,
To win his spouse's rapture, builded these,
Causing the world to marvel and to cry :
" Hail to great Babylon, the queen of towns ! "

Here played the queen with maidens from her land,
Jeweled with breastplates and tiaras rare,
And with her birds, and gems, and amulets,
She dreamed of glory and Summúramit,
Besprent with star-shaped ornaments to show
Her origin divine was from the stars,
She being the daughter of a Midian king.
And as she mused she heard the soldiers sing
Upon the parapets far, far below.

CHORUS OF BABYLONIAN WARRIORS.

We are perfumed, sleek and curled,
We, the terror of the world,
And we march upon our bastions blowing trumpets of defiance.
We have only one desire,
To press on through blood and fire,
And in Moloch the majestic we have absolute reliance.

Like comets shine our shields
When we rush upon the fields ;
There on earth exists no nation that would dare to show
resistance
When our startling battle-cries
Rise in fury to the skies,
When we fight with heavy lances and the gods' sublime
assistance.

We are dreaded far and wide ;
Of the King we are the pride,
And our fame has spread and ripened in each province and
each village ;

And the traitor's native ground
Shakes and trembles at the sound
Of our coming for the challenge, for the combat, for the
    pillage !

Our long terrifying darts
Hotly pierce the rebel hearts ;
Even great Nineveh, our sister, as a proverb hails our valor.
We have jeweled troops of horse
When we charge through town in force,
And our shields of brass like mirrors e'er reflect the foeman's
    pallor.

In our lofty zigurats,
Idly dreaming on our mats,
When peace reigns in the dominion and the city burns with
    pleasure,
We recall with fierce delight
The last echoes of the fight,
And the captured shields and horses of the enemy we treasure.

Oh great Merodach, appear !
We are worn of rusting here ;
Lead us onward toward the Shuhites, who in strife were beaten
    never ;

O'er their pastures green and wide
Let us insolently ride,
And with spear, and dart, and chariot let us crush them down
forever !

SCENE III.

And lo ! one hundred prisoners of war,
Taken at Memphis fighting for their King,
Who cared for them as he would care for sand,
And who refused to ransom them with gold,
Were led in corded couples to be slain ;
And to their honor be it now proclaimed
That not one passed with hot or weeping eyes.
Some prayed to Isis to protect their lives,
But they were bowmen and cared naught for death,
And if the god were silent, they would die
Without a murmur, praising Pharaoh still.

Now many dreamed that a strong whirring lance,
Hurled at their breasts, would seek and find their hearts,
Or that an arrow dancing through the air
Would sink within their foreheads, nothing more.

But when they reached the quarter for their tombs,
They saw in anguish that one hundred poles
With ropes and iron bands awaited them,
And that a warrior's death they could not claim.

The crowds grew dense and turbulent, until
Each man of Egypt had been firmly bound
Unto the pole erected for his woe,
And then one hundred archers left the ranks
And put their eyes out with a rush of spears,
While, as they fell all bloody to the ground,
The dogs of Babylon crunched them in their jaws.

Dead were the wretches not, and many men
Skilled in the art of torture now appeared,
And, cutting with sharp iron long layers of skin,
They flayed alive these unprotected ones ;
Ay, with such wondrous craft that not one died,
Although they spat on the tormentor's brows,
And for this sign of wrath their tongues were clipped
While people were allowed to hasten near
And probe their skinless breasts with jagged stones.

Then they were left to broil within the sun,
And keep sweet love for Pharoah in their hearts,

Who, with rich wines, and honey, and fair girls,
Was dreaming by the lotus of the Nile.
And at the set of sun four-score were dead,
While on the morrow three still clung to life,
And these were taken and hurled into a pit,
There finding speedy death by adder's fangs,
While laughing multitudes with shining spades
Poured the hot sand upon them, even so.

THE TEMPLE.

The beacon fire blazed from the tower of Bel,
The tower held sacred to the highest priest,
And lo! the incense and the fragrant wood
Rose in sweet vapor to the attendant gods,
And filled their mighty nostrils with delight.
The brazen tripod holder of such scent
Was holy unto them ; they granted prayers,
Caused rain, gave children, victory and gold
To their obedient city, dutiful.
Yea, and he blessed the fountains and the doves
Within the temple's courts, and even came
Invisible behind the crimson silk
That curtained their choice shrine, and calmly gazed
Upon the lotus woven thereon in gold ;
And often, calling to the dazzled priest
Burning delicious santal at their feet,
Would bid him summon from the vineyards near
Some favored maid who sold the city grapes,
And guide her trembling limbs with surest hand,
Among the man-faced lions of the court,

Unto his shrine, and there be fond with her,
All for his glory, for the priest's delight
Would satisfy the cravings of the god !
And so it came to pass when Beltis spake,
For, if the maid was sweet and loved her god,
She was to gain an ell of Tyrian silk,
A silver lute, and have her choice of doves.
Then would the dull-eyed eunuchs bear her home
And leave her, happy, fertile by her god,
Exempt forever from Mylitta's law.

Here of the gods were all the shrines and altars
Blending with gold, with crimson, silk and marble.
Here the great planetary gods, in number
Seven, and only seven, were humbly worshiped :
Adar and Nergal, Merodach with Nebo,
Ishtar and Bel, and Anu the all-holy.
While in the sacred cincture of the temple,
Perfumed and flowerful, stood the sacred statues
Of Shamas, the god of light and all things beauteous,
Of Abitur, the lord of hills and mountains,
Of Moloch, god of war and devastation,
Of El, a king of gods, the god of thunder ;
And near him, gods eleven, who obeyed him,
Although they also were high gods in heaven.

Here were the deathless spirits of heaven, three hundred,
Adored with cries, and blood, and genuflections,
Ay, and of earth six hundred perfect spirits,
With Mulgè, god of under-worlds, their master,
And Hea, lord of earth and king of rivers.
Unto great Vul, the god of rain, a clamor
Rose from the people, for the fields were arid
In distant valleys of the mighty Empire,
And, though they lived in bounteous abundance,
Their hearts grew sore to think of starving brothers.

Then came sweet maidens praying unto Beltis,
With choruses of praise and tinkling timbrels,
Hailing the great god Ashtaroth, who near her
Breathed upon earth the spirit of all beauty ;
For he was crowned with stars and lord of serpents.
To eagle-headed Nisroch came the warriors,
Fresh from a hundred fields of bestial carnage,
And hailed him and his neighbor god, fierce Dagon.
Yea, and they hailed Bel-shar-uzzur's sweet mother,
Nitocris fair and radiant as the sunrise,
Beloved of El and Bel, the lords of Sumia,
Beloved of Gulè, the serene sun-goddess,
And of sweet Sin, the lustrous, loving moon-god.

Then, having bowed before the lofty rulers,
The people, trembling as the grass in tempests,
Came to a shrine above all others holy,
The emblem of some awful power superior
To fate and to eternity, an essence
Symbolical, omnipotent and mystic,
Vaguely expressed by one great golden circle
Encompassed by a wheel of wings angelic !

Then toward the statue of immortal Vul
Five hundred scented priests with solemn tread
Marched, bearing lambs for slaughter, and much spice,
And at his altars' grees made pause and sang :

CHORUS TO VUL.

Our robes are flounced, oh Vul ! our caps are horned ;
For thy sweet sake with flowers we have adorned
      Our flanks.
We are one thousand who unto thee give,
While thou, supreme, dost deign to let us live,
      Our thanks.

Our cheeks are rubbed with pumice, and our arms
Are naked kept, to celebrate thy charms;
      Our wrists
Are palsied by our bracelets, and we guide
Lovers unto thy shrine, and guard with pride
      Their trysts.

Our sandals are embroidered, and the white
Of all our gowns rivals Ishtar's at night,
      And deep
Within our breast thy mystic lotus-flower,
Emblem divine of thy divinest power,
      We keep.

Upon our fillets and our ear-rings' gold,
The mystic circle graven there behold
      Of Fate.
We worship thee with many harps and reeds,
For early thou attendest to our needs,
      And late.

Saban the eunuch guards thy sacred shrine
And, doing so, is sacred and divine
      To all;

For we arise when in the noiseless night
We hear in tones that even Kallassan fright,
Thy call !

Great Vul ! we stand here robed to please thee now ;
Blood spilt for thee is clotted on our brow,
Oh Vul !
Thy presence we have summoned, thrills and awes ;
Favor us, Wonder ! and Death's sternest laws
Annul !

The city knew the king had deigned to bathe
In lake Nitocris for his mother's sake,
For twenty slaves had filled the lake with spice,
And delicious herbs, and many loads of flowers,
And Sethos, the good man who bore his cup,
Had passed the city's gates with fruit and wine,
And armed attendant guarded the king's gems,
For he wore gold and rubies when he bathed.

The holder of the royal parasol
Stood in the sun, and then the envied guard
Who bore the shield of great Bel-shar-uzzúr
Appeared, and with him hosts of shining men,

Leading the banners of great Merodach,
And horses burdened by their straps of gold,
And many chariots armed with iron scythes.
The royal tent, tufted with ostrich plumes,
Was carried by fair women to the bath,
And in it they reposed on scented mats
To give the monarch pleasure by their limbs.
And lo ! the trumpets sounded, and the lyres
For the great king, mighty Bel-shar-uzzúr,
Entered the chariot with bejeweled feet,
While all the people bowed unto the dust.
And at the sight men slew themselves with joy,
And this was told unto the king, who smiled
And bade the corpses to be natroned well
For swift interment in the city's vaults,
The price thereof to come from his own purse.

SCENE IV.

Then, with dark locks all filleted and spiced,
A dainty harlot boldly sauntered by,
With pretty shoulder-shrugs to please the crowds,
And tempting undulations of the hips,

And singing as she went inspiring songs
That lured the callow students from their doors,
Who greeted her with ribald words and strolled
Back to their cellars, for they had no gold,
And, lacking gold, they could possess her not.
Therefore they hated their superior's wealth,
And sneered at Vul, who would not give them love,
Ay, cursed the gods who left them without coin.

Heedless of this young lust, the harlot passed,
Imperious, crying: "Give me bricks of gold,
Or galbanum, or precious gems, and then
I will do for thee what to all I do !
I will revere thee as a god by night,
If thou art strong and if thou ownest gold !"
Then, pausing, with her lovely eyes aflame,
She wove a wreath of roses, singing thus :

SONG.

Oh Mylitta ! hear my prayer !
Send me lovers rich and fair,
For I languish in desertion and my bosom pants for pleasure :
And to thank thee with all zeal,
In the temple I will kneel,
And will bring thee spice and ointments, and a portion of my
    treasure.

Thou, who gazest from the stars,
Thou, whose glory nothing mars,
Take sweet pity on thy servant, who in wanton pride obeys
    thee.
To do honor to thy feast
I have given my flesh to priests,
To the priests my lips deserted, but in sacrifice to praise thee.

By thy beauty I am graced,
Yet the city's ways I traced
Many times since fall of sunlight, and I find no compensation.

All the warriors have smiled,

By my loveliness beguiled,

But the king has held their payment, and their looks are
hesitation.

Oh Mylitta! for thy sake,

When to dawn mine eyes did wake,

I made purchase of sweet unguents and red roses for my tresses.

In mine eyes there lurks the fire

Of unquenchable desire,

Yet the striplings of the city spurn my beauty and caresses.

Oh Mylitta! goddess sweet,

I have lingered at thy feet,

In the temple's shrine mysterious with thy priestesses ecstatic ;

I have given to them my breast,

When by hunger sore oppressed,

To appease thy righteous rancor in thy garments emblematic.

I have roses in my hair,

My white breast is oiled and bare,

I have kisses warm and cunning to excite a youth to sue me.

Oh Mylitta! hear my prayer,

And send lovers rich and fair,

With silk robes, or gold, or spices, ere the morn awakens to me !

And for thee in swift return,

For a day I will sojourn

In the temple as the plaything of the bearded priests audacious,

And when sighing in their arms,

I will praise thy wondrous charms,

And will sing thee songs of rapture, oh Mylitta! white and

gracious!

Then from the swaying crowd an agéd man,

A Ninevite, so reckoned by his curls,

Broke loose and stopped the harlot with his hand,

Placing a bit of silver in her breast,

And to her tent she guided him, while all

Watched them with envy glaring in their eyes.

Deep in the labyrinth of Bit-Saggath,

In dismal vaults illumed by flickering lamps,

The skilled Embalmers of far Egypt work,

And, toiling, sing loud praises of themselves.

CHORUS OF SKILLED EMBALMERS FROM EGYPT.

We toil within the temple's crypts, with ghastly dead beside us,
The horrors of our handiwork from people oft divide us,
And yet we all are merry men, right fond of jest and laughter,
And, being bosom friends of Death, we fear not the hereafter.
From corpses stark we draw the brains, and cleanse with drugs
      delicious,
We purge the emptied bodies clean of mortal soilure vicious,
With costly palm-wine, sweetest oil and perfumes aromatic,
And fill the spirit of the clay with gratitude ecstatic.

We place within the silent flesh bruised myrrh, and salt, and
      spices,
Then press in natron seventy days, and while it rests, devices
Of subtle kind and rarest art we fashion for the mourners,
And all great Babylon knows well that we are skilled adorners.
When ready for our nimble touch, the litheness of our fingers,
Again the perfumed solid flesh in our deep work-house lingers,

And, smeared with gum and bandaged well, we place it in our
  cases,
And decorate with images of gods, and flowers, and places.
So, upright it is given to those who all it's worth did cherish,
To rest within its sepulcher until the earth shall perish !

Within the bandages we lay papyri, glass and agate,
To serve the dead on some far day and guard him from the
   maggot ;
And scarabei, and amulets, with rings and bracelets golden,
We place beside the withered palms as is the custom olden,
For only bodies of the poor when washed, and boiled, and
  salted,
In common wood, in common clay, go up to the Exalted.
Of sacred animals we clean the crocodiles and lizards,
And send them to our temples vast for sale to priests and
   wizards,
With natroned fish and ibises, with serpents, apes and cattle,
And many a valiant warrior's horse that neighed out blood in
   battle.
We have perfumed the holy bulls, and many a cat and vulture
Will live until the world doth fall and by our fingers' culture,
And many dogs, and many rams, with curléd asps and foxes,
Remain immortal in their sleep within our scented boxes.

While in the mammoth temple overhead,
Whose pillars pierce the very flanks of heaven,
Old, withered men, grim guardians of the scrolls,
And manuscripts, and archives of the gods,
Stammer with toothless mouths, and feebly whine
Strange cadences to Assur-báni-pal.

CHORUS.

Hail, hail to Assur-báni-pal the great,
  Whose fame was guarded by a people jealous !
Hail to the kings he labored to create !
  Hail to his mages in their worship zealous !
Hail to his reign in Nineveh, where came
  To bow the knee the sovereigns he created,
Ay, from his lips a simple word to claim,
  And leave in fear and trembling, but elated !
Hail to the puissant and all-holy name
  Of Necho, king of Memphis, stern and powerful !
And Pisan-hor, who could the lions tame,
  Near Natho, his great city walled and towerful !
Hail to Pagruru, of far Pisupt king !
  And Pukkimanin-hapi of Athribis,
Hail and revere him as a holy thing ;
  Bow in the dust before his sword and ibis.

Great Assur-báni-pal, years, years ago,
  Made Nech-ke king of Henins in his glory,

And Petubastes summond by his bow
  At Tanis reigned until his brows grew hoary.
Hail, hail! he sent Unamunu the fair
  To Natho as his humble lord and vassal,
And Sheshonk to Busiris, even there
  To live in fat, and plenty, and in wassail.
Iptikhardesu he did deign to send
  To far Pazatti-hurunpi Ku's palace,
To be its king and force all foes to bend,
  Foes ever filled with hostile hate and malice.
And Necht-hor-ansini of Pi-sabdnût
  In ways imperious cherished and upheld him,
And in his temples, Zika of Siyout
  The fattest brutes in sacrifices felled him.
Hail, hail to Assur-báni-pal the great!
  Mark on your tablets' clay in writing mystic
How Lamintu to Chemmis draped in state
  Brought to his people offerings cabalistic,
And hail to Assur-báni-pal, for he
  Sent Munti-Manche to the Theban city!
Hail to his triumph over land and sea!
  Hail to his grace, his valor and his pity!

  Bel-shar-uzzúr, returning from the bath,
  Thinks of the gods within the walls of Bel,

And can remember that he has not prayed
For hours eleven ; therefore he commands
His hosts to halt before the sacred shrines,
And, as he has but paltry time to waste,
And yet must all propitiate, he cries
Unto his herald : "Call grave Kalassan,
And bid the flouncéd priests in solemn ways
Pray for their king the war god Merodach,
And likewise tender worship unto El,
And unto Hea, Nisroch, and to Sin ! "
For see, the king is weary of the bath,
And he is fain with sleep to kill an hour.
Pray for him, priests ! And lo ! the priests obeyed,
And, as Bel-shar-uzzúr returned in state
To taste the kisses of a favorite slave
Caught in the snowy mountains of the north,
A woman with long tresses touched with gold,
Who lured his wasting fancies by her charm,
The roar of sacerdotal lungs arose.

CHORUS OF PRIESTS.

Great Merodach, first-born of gods, we hail thee !
We slay with fire the foes that dare assail thee !
  Oh, mighty god of war and desolation !
    In thee there dwells no pity and no error.
    Thy glance is death, thy very name is terror,
  Thy touch is flame, thy breath extermination !

Great Hea, lord of all the earth, we praise thee !
Spice-burning altars we forever raise thee.
  Thou art the god majestic of all rivers,
    And in our sacred violet robes we wonder
    When overhead we hear thy ominous thunder,
  When mighty Babylon in stupor quivers !

Great El, of gods the highest, we adore thee !
In deep humility we bow before thee.
  Thou art the lord of Sumir green and flowerful ;
    Thou reignest pure above the earth's affliction ;
    Thy voice is one of peace and benediction ;
  We hail thy august shadow, calm and powerful !

Great Sin ! before thine altars rot the corses
Of hundreds captured by our armored forces,
  And from the moon, where thou dost have thy dwelling,
    Thou canst look down and canst behold the gory
    And withered heads that now attest thy glory,
  And hear thy praise through twenty temples swelling !

Prodigious Bin ! god of the deafening thunder
And all the gems that in the world lie under,
  Protect us from the insolence of foemen ;
    Blight with thy breath the curses that distress us ;
    With fertile fields and heavy harvests bless us ;
  Disclose thy presence by some sudden omen !

Stupendous Dagon ! god of waves and fishes,
Harken, we pray thee, to our humble wishes ;
  Fill thy true people's nets with rare provision ;
    Save from the havoc of the angry waters
    The labors of our city's sons and daughters,
  And we can taunt the storm-fiend in derision !

And, oh Mylitta ! in sweet generation
We beg of thee to multiply our nation ;
  Let not our supple maidens perish sterile ;

Guard them, thy chosen, from the fiends infernal ;
May they grow fructuous as the meadows vernal ;
And save their beauty from the city's peril.

And thou, oh Nisroch ! thou, the eagle-headed,
Thou, the malignant wonder, stern and dreaded,
Guard us from sin and from all disaffection ;
Upon bare knees we worship thee as holy ;
In thee our faith is ever centered solely ;
Grant us, great god, thy treasureful protection !

Then, like a wind that bursts in a simoom,
The royal archers, passing through the gates,
Rushed quickly toward the temple, for they hoped
To hail the king and thunder forth their praise ;
For they knew well how he admired their songs.
So, singing in their rancous soldier way,
They told their prowess to the listening town,
Forever gladdened when these favorites passed.

SONGS OF ARCHERS.

We are the strong archers,
The wonderful marchers,
Who pass through the fields with a rattle of quivers;
The god Bin protects us,
His thunder delects us,
The blood of our foes stains the foam of our rivers!

Their hosts are confounded
By terror unbounded,
When singing we pass in our armor defiant;
At Memphis's battle
We slew them like cattle,
And trod them to dust with the steps of a giant!

Our limbs are athletic,
Our war-cry frenetic,
Our spears by the priests have been made talismanic:
Wherever they glisten,
The foes in fear listen
And fly for the shelter of towns in their panic.

Our king has admired us,
His smile has inspired us,
He hails at Bit-Saggath our prowesses yearly ;
He can call us his glorious
Brave soldiers victorious,
And oft at our valor he marvels sincerely.

The insolent Cissions,
By sins and omissions,
Are now his vile slaves, with their children and houses ;
And oft does he praise us,
And flatter and daze us
By words of great cheer when he sings and carouses.

The Elamites' city
We sacked without pity ;
Its gods and its warriors could never withstand us ;
Our death-dealing arrows
Were swifter than sparrows,
And Moloch and Merodach deigned to command us.

We are the strong archers,
The wonderful marchers,
Who pass through the fields with a rattle of quivers ;

(15)

The god Bin protects us,
His thunder delects us,
The blood of our foes stains the foam of our rivers

Bel-shar-uzzur, as curious as a child,
Entered the gardens where his beasts were fed ;
For he was proud of animals and birds,
Loving them more than women and than men.
And slaves walked with him, bearing meat and fruit
To throw unto his pets as he desired.
And there were seventy lions in a pit,
Roaring with hunger, and the monarch laughed
And bade a slave, Assarapac by name,
One who that morn had broken a sontal face,
To leap into the pit.
                    The craven bowed
His dooméd head in dust and shrieked for grace,
But there was none, and as he failed to leap,
Headlong they cast him down amid the brutes,
And ere his body sank upon the sand,
The ravenous monsters gnawned it to red shreds.

This pleased the king, and to his guard he said :
" Have others of my household proved amiss ? "

And no one spake, until a soldier said :
" No, mighty king, their duty has been done."
And this he said because he lived on quails,
On fat and Eschol wine, and he was fond
Of jests and music, and his soul was good,
Because his body was as sleek as oil.

Then did the king throw fruitage to his goats,
And pullets to the foxes in their lairs,
And his great bears he pelted with rich sweets,
Laughing to see them smell the perfumed ground
And lick up gravel with the sticky meats.

The crocodiles that spawned within the Nile,
Gift of Ægyptia's king, he likewise fed
With human flesh, or with a live gazelle,
And many a deer, and to his grunting boars
He threw sweet nuts and acorns with his hand,
Laughing and grinning like a chubby babe.

And one flamingo, one he loved the most,
Was ill, its neck all ruffled by a lynx.
Therefore he placed it in the vipers' hole ;
The horned cerastes, a most deadly thing,
Which bit the bird and eyed it growing cold.

Then the great king made visit to his lynx,
His petted lynx, chained to a cage of gold,
And fed from golden dishes ; but his wolves
Had brazen dishes only, like the dogs,
And these he fed with many living birds,
Fat quails and bitterns, geese and porcupines,
And he grew merry at the slaughter there,
And bade four slaves to lie upon the soil
Until the elephants his father trained
Approached to stamp their lives out with huge feet,
For this delighted him and all the court.

Then, as he rambled through the green pastures,
He came unto his panthers lithe and fierce,
Who glared upon him with grave golden eyes ;
And these he fed with camel flesh and rats,
And jerboa meat and ibexes alive,
While his hyenas snorted for their share ;
But they were filthy things and had to starve
Until each second day, when Jews were slain,
And them they could devour like stinking beasts.

Now, as the king was weary and amort,
He bade his slaves tie two fat beavers up

And hurl them in a pit where leopards glared ;
And it was done, while from the parapet
He watched the supple monsters fiercely gorge.

Around the brazen porches of the town
Huge obelisks were dragged by panting men,
To grace the lanes and highways of the realm,
And all were slaves captured in Theban sands,
Who still revered their king and loved their gods.
And when their masters, weary of the sun
That smote their faces, lingered in the shade,
Forgetting that their goads were idle, yea,
When the taskmasters loitered near the gates
To purchase water from a gum-girl fair
Or dally with a harlot in the trench,
Then, in their flowing mother-tongue, beloved
And idolized of them, they would repeat
This dolorous appeal with humid eyes :

CHORUS OF EGYPTIAN PRISONERS.

Oh ! we can remember the melons and vetches
   That grew in our sunny and beautiful land,
Before the impure Babylonian wretches
   Had covered our armies with cerements of sand !

Yea, we can remember the palm-crownéd vases,
   With rivulets running more beautiful far
Than all the broad plains and the meadow-grown places
   That girdle this town to the end of Shinar.

We think of our gods and our temples deserted,
   Still glorious without us, while here we are slaves ;
We go to our labor with damp eyes averted,
   And dream of the spot of our ancestors' graves.

No more shall we see in its silvery splendor
   The glittering rush of the fall of the Nile ;
No more shall we hurry to crush the offender,
   No more shall we bask in our sovereign's smile.

For Ammon, the king of all gods, has betrayed us,
  And Knuphis, the god of oases, seems dead ;
They sullenly let the Assyrian invade us,
  And yet we will worship no gods in their stead !

Great Ptah with the cat, ever holy, as symbol,
  And Khem, god of nature, has left us in woe,
Though often our feet and our fingers were nimble
  To praise him with dances and harps long ago !

Oh Isis ! Osiris ! oh Ptah ! do not leave us
  To fruitlessly perish in agony here !
The gods of Assyria mock and deceive us !
  Their mercy far more than their anger we fear !

Oh Nepti, thou mother of gods far above us !
  Oh Ra, mighty sun we adore in the day !
Oh Thoth of the Ibis, who promised to love us !
  Oh Min of the sunlight, pray lead us away !

Hail Pasht and Anieké, Maut, Tafné and Horus !
  Hail Athor and Savak ! In you we still trust !
Oh, join giant voices in one mighty chorus,
  And level foul Babylon down to the dust !

And as they toiled and sweated with their bricks,
Fainting from fever when the stone rebelled,
A long procession of the city's dames,
All garlanded with lotus and sweet flowers,
With leather amulets upon their breasts,
Passed in unto the temple's square, where towered
The enormous golden phalli wreathed with leaves,
And on their tops communed a bearded priest,
Such was the law, for seven days and nights,
Such was the fashion of the Zir-basiet.
And all the women gazed upon the gold
And sang with fervor as they placed their wreaths:

PHALLIC SONG.

Oh, thrice holy and delightful golden phallus!
  Now before thee in dumb ecstasy we kneel ;
To our prayers and supplications be not callous.
  Mighty Vul, whose sign we worship with all zeal !

We have bathed our bodies pure in the Araxes,
  To be fairer and more supple at thy rites,
For the ardor in our bodies stronger waxes,
  And we long to know thy sweet voluptuous nights !

Listen, Vul ! unto our lyre's serene vibrations ;
  Make us fertile as the blossoms on the plain ;
Grant us pleasure much and exquisite sensations ;
  Let thy kisses fall upon us like a rain !

For behold thy glorious phallus decked and flowerful,
  With a star of gold that glitters far above,
And behold our lamps that burn beneath, Oh powerful,
  Ever holy god that lives and breathes in love.

Here in monstrous Bit-Saggath, thy temple splendid,
　We adore thee with the timbrel's silvery noise,
And we beg of thee until our lives are ended
　Sweet continuance of all warm and fleshly joys !

For, oh Vul ! thou art the symbol of creation,
　And sweet Beltis is thy consort white and warm,
And we worship thee with passion's exultation
　In the beauty of thy gold-terrestrial form !

We have amulets that bear thy sign engraven,
　And when ardors burn upon our bosoms bare,
In thy temple we can find a precious haven,
　And are cloyed by all the sweetness hidden there.

Oh thrice holy, all-delightful golden phallus !
　Hover o'er us when we toil and when we dream ;
Haunt our humble home and haunt our monarch's palace,
　And upon us all shower down thy gifts supreme !

　A priest of Nebo, the great god supreme,
　A priest whose mouth was warm with flowery words
　And lovely phrasings of his mother tongue,
　Gentle and supple, twisted like a reed
　By his fair fancy, in the temple rose

And taught the children, who assembled there,
Some of the signs of worship of the gods.
In Chaldee, the sweet idiom of the town,
He spake to them, and told them seven stars,
Five planets and the sun, yea, and the moon,
Timed the advance of this the fertile earth
To heavenly music, by no mortal heard.
He told them of the brilliant thirty stars
That were revered and called " consulting gods,"
And how twelve stars that shimmered in the north,
And others, twelve, that burned within the south,
Compelled the destinies of live and dead
And were revered as " Judges of the World."

And as he burned sweet spices at the shrines,
He told them that the months were sacred all,
And bade them learn to cherish and repeat
Their names and hold them holy in their hearts.
Therefore the children sang with treble tones :

" Hail to the month of Nisan, the month of Anu and
      Bel !
And hail to Hea the fair, who rules all the month Iyyar !
Hail to the month of Sivan, belonging of right to Sin !

And hail to the month Tammuz, of
Ninip the lawful month !
Hail to the month of Elul, the
Month of the Queen Ishtàr !
And also to Tisri, hail, the month of Shamos, the god !
Hail to fair Marchesvăn, great
Merodach's holy month !
Hail to the month of Kislev, to
Nergal made sacred now !
And hail to Tebat, the month of
Papsukul famed and great !
And hail to Sebat, the month the chosen of amorous
    Vul !
And hail to the month of gods, the seven great gods
    Adar !
And hail to the month Veadar, the month of the fathers
    of gods ! "

SCENE V.

PART I.

Lo, through full twenty gates came charioteers,
Laden with spoil and treasure for the king,
With horses belled and cinctured in rare silk,
Escorted by fierce bowmen mailed in iron,

With maces on their backs and blinding shields.
And adroit slingers to protect the wealth ;
For there was onyx, and much amethyst
From out the land of Belad, and they brought
Chalcedony and alabaster, too,
With ebony and jasper from Tabit,
And lapis-lazuli from Kedin town,
Likewise from Karid and from walled Anat,
Gifts for the king, who, lavish with his gold,
Would place them in his lapidaries' palms
And bid them rub and polish till the stones
Were worthy of the king, Bel-shar-uzzúr.

PART II.

Now in the city was a gentle maid,
  Alca by name, who whiled away the hours
  Petting her birds and weaving wreathes of flowers
Within her father's dwelling, in the shade.

He was a warrior stationed on the walls,
  And gave his daughter his large share of spoil,
  So that her dainty fingers might not toil,
So that she might spill perfume in her halls.

And she was pure, and no intrepid youth
Had lured her fancy by a glittering gem ;
    Nor had a beard been pressed unto her hem,
    Nor had she lingered in a merchant's booth.

And she was beautiful, with ebon hair
    Scented and braided with new fillets, and
    She wore a jasper signet on her hand,
And roses in her bosom round and fair.

Yet she was wise and knew that Beltis claimed
    Her beauteous body in the temple's shrine,
    For one sweet night of ecstasy divine ;
Yea, this she knew, and yet was unashamed.

And all her heart was bursting with young pride,
    For she, the humble maiden, white and pure,
    Had once beheld the king, Bel-shar-uzzúr,
Pass in his chariot on the bastions wide.

And he had gazed upon her as he passed,
    Ay, the great king ! and this sweet knowledge sent
    A sense of joy and much bewilderment
Through her warm flesh and made her heart beat fast.

The time was nigh when she would have to pass
   Within the temple to await the gold
   Of any passing stranger, and enfold
His body with her jeweled arms, alas !

And this annoyed her soul, because her love
   Was pledged to Ammarac, a warrior tall,
   Who was her pride, her passion and her all,
Strong as a god and humble as a dove.

And through the sultry day, when he would come
   To sit and sing beside her in the shade,
   She longed to be another than a maid,
And passions woke and triumphed that were dumb.

And, lo ! he spake to her, and softly said :
   " When to the temple thou art taken in state,
   Fear naught, sweet Alca, do not hesitate ;
I will be there ; harbor no evil dread.

" Thy ransom-coin will be of graven gold,
   And I will press it in thy furtive palm,
   Then I can fearless taste thy kisses' balm,
And all the whiteness of thy body hold !

"That brutal Tammac, who pursues thee now
　　With gifts of ointment and great lustful sighs,
　　With braided beard and hot and swinish eyes,
Will never touch the fillets of thy brow.

"Thou shalt be mine, and I will love thee much,
　　And prove my love in manly loving ways.
　　Mine ears shall reap the harvest of thy praise,
When thou dost pant to Vul beneath my touch!"

And Alca smiled and kissed his bearded face,
　　Saying: "'Tis well! Thy whim I will obey,
　　And I shall wait thy coming on that day,
When the vast temple shelters my disgrace!"

Then she arose, and placing milk and fruit
　　With spicy gums before him, she reclined
　　Upon her silks, and to becalm his mind
She summoned forth the spirit of her lute.

And he was tame, and lingered at her feet,
　　Kissing her limbs and toying with her hair;
　　For there was peace and much contentment there,
And all his dreams were fruitful and complete.

The sacred daylight broke, and Alca, draped
In lovely garments and her choicest gems,
Entered the temple of Mylitta, where
She took her place amid a thousand maids,
There to await the coming of the coin.
And in the scented gloom she could discern,
Vaguely at first, and lucidly at last,
A cluster of women who had had no coin,
Ay, women who had lingered there for years,
Hopelessly captives till the silver came!
And some were young, but marked by moles or scars,
And some were old and spake with wrinkled cheeks,
And Alca pitied them and cried : "O Bel !
I pray to thee that I may ne'er be thus ! "
While, as she prayed, the women who were spurned
Circled the altar, and in desolate tones
Sang to the god who had not heard their prayers :

> "Oh ! will no great warrior stern
> To allure us hence return ?
> Must we now remain forever in the temple's halls prodigious ?
> We have faces white and fair,
> With keen eyes and lustrous hair,
> And with fervor we have yielded to all rites and rules religious,

(10)

" Yet in vain we stretch our hand,
And with faltering voice demand
The bright salvatory silver that will save us from this prison !
Yet full many a gentle maid,
In enticing silks arrayed,
From her corner near the altar for long years has not arisen !

" Oh Mylitta ! in the might
Of thy all-absorbing light,
See us bow before thine altars, slaves of love, and law, and duty !
Let us gaze but once again
On the lovely leafy plain,
Take us hence ere Time rapacious hurls its javelin at our beauty !

" We are sacred as the sun,
And our task we dare not shun,
Yet in vain we tempt the comers with alert, voluptuous glances !
Must we linger here and die,
As the solemn years go by,
And lose pleasure, hope and beauty, and the joy of wines and
    dances ?

" Even thy priests, who boil and burn
With all lechery, will turn

From our naked bosoms tempting, knowing death is swift and
    certain,
        If they fall from thy high grace
        By one unallowed embrace
On our lips or on our bodies near the sacred altar's curtain.

        " Oh great queen of night, Ashtar !
        That in heaven dost shine afar,
We are dying for deliverance and the frenzy of caresses !
        Deign to send our spirit gleams
        Of a hope to light our dreams,
And thy name will be unto us as a balm that soothes and
    blesses ! "

But no bright coin was dropped upon their laps,
And no one even paused to market them.

Vast crowds assembled at the temple's gates,
Awaiting entrance when the doors unbarred
Should give to all an enviable choice
Of supple flesh and animated eyes ;
And Ammarac was present, with a bit
Of flashing gold held firmly in his hand,

Destined for Alca, and his bosom leaped
When thoughts of love went soaring through his heart,
Thoughts of her nudity and drooping eyes,
Thoughts of the rich allurement of her breasts.

Impatient, ardent, he stood waiting there,
While the grave priests, heedless of his desire,
Exasperating, in their scented cloaks,
Sang unto Bel, as if the massive doors
Were destined never to be flung apart :

CHORUS OF PRIESTS.

Before thee, Bel, we bow !
The glory of thy brow
   Doth light us.
Thou art of gods supreme,
And thou in ways extreme
   Canst smite us !

To dye thine altars red
For thee our foes have bled
   And perished !
Thy power that never failed
Is through our city hailed
   And cherished !

Oh. Lord of great Accad !
We strive to make thee glad
   With treasure,
And by thy power the sky,
The sun and moon on high
   We measure.

Within our naked breasts
Our ardor never rests ;
        We love thee;
And know that by the sun
Of gods there can be none
        Above thee !

We are the seventy priests
Who guard thy rites and feasts,
        Who hail thee !
We deal thy lightning blows
On one and all, when foes
        Assail thee !

We bend before thee, Bel,
Thou only canst dispel
        Our sorrow !
And on our weary knees
Wisdom from thy decrees
        We borrow !

Thou art of gods supreme,
Thy hand in ways extreme
        Can smite us !

Hail ! for we humbly bow ;
The glory of thy brow
Doth light us !

Then, as they ceased, the doors were opened wide,
But, ere tall Ammarac with brawny arms
Could reach his chosen one, although he clove
The brows of twenty eaten up by lust,
Who yearned to pick the fairest in the place,
He was forestalled by Tammac, who had dropped
A bit of gold in wondering Alca's lap,
Saying : " Mylitta prosper thee, sweet maid ! "
And every one had seen the deed performed,
And forty priests protected Tammac there,
Crying : " It is the law ! The maid is his !
The man was hiding in the temple, true,
The deed is fraud, but sacred must remain ;
The woman for the rite to him belongs."
They spake, yet as they spake the priests knew not
That grave Kalastan, the superior priest,
Had taken bribes of ninety golden bricks
To let hot Tammac enter unperceived,
And Ammarac was hooted from the place.

Then, like a bustard darting on a dove,
Tammac seized Alca in his virile arms,
And he was fain to drag her to a vault,
When, lo! shrill trumpets sounded, and a voice
Rang through the temple : "Lo! our beauteous king,
The heavenly king, Bel-shar-uzzúr, is here!"
And it was true, because the king appeared,
Asking the reasons of such tumult there.
Then Alca tore herself from Tammac's hold,
And kneeling to the king cried out : "Oh King!
Thou once didst gaze upon me in the street,
And that one glance is treasured in my loins!
Save me!   This thing is fraudulent and false!
This man was couchant in the temple ere
The doors were opened!   Save me, gentle king!
For I would rather soil my bed with toads
Than yield my body to his scented touch!"
And the king gazed upon her and said naught,
Watching the undulations of her breast,
Gazed till the blushes scarleted her face,
Then, waving back the hordes of angry priests,
He bade four eunuchs bear the girl away,
And take her to his palace, there to live
Until the matter had been legalized.

And all the people shouted with delight,
O'erjoyed to see the grave intolerant priests
Bearded at last by the all-holy king !

Bel-shar-uzzúr, within his sacred room,
Held Alca dazzled by his regal glance ;
Speechless she saw the scintillating flame
Of furious passion in his god-blest eyes !
Yet he, the king, the glory of the earth,
Dared not to press her beauty to his lips.
He, lord of myriads, at that very hour
Was powerless to break the laws of gods,
And for an empire he could kiss her not,
And this he knew, and cried aloud : "Poor king !
Even I am limited, the son of gods ! "
And, as he mused, there came a noise of brass
Stricken by brass unto his idle ear,
And from the window he could see below
A thousand priests, who by the sign of Bel
Had paralyzed the watchman of the courts,
And called upon the monarch to appear,
For the priests' vengeance is a fearful thing.

And he came forth, knowing the rigid laws,
And cried : "Ye driveling fools and dogs, be still !

Bel doth protect you, and I know his wish !
I, the great king, I, the beloved of Bel,
Will bow before his will, but not at yours !
This girl shall go unto her righteous lord,
Young Tammac, for an hour.   The king has said !
So get ye hence !   Within a hurried hour
She, guarded by my spears, shall go to you !"
And, turning to the trembling maid, he cried :
"Sweet maiden, for the gods thou must obey,
And be the toy of Tammac for an hour ;
But I shall wipe thy stain away in blood !"
And, summoning a host of archers near,
He bade them march as escort to the maid,
And in his chariot of war he rode
Unto the temple.

      And it came to pass
That Alca, led into a rosy bower
By priests commissioned for this very task,
Was given up to Tammac, while in bands
The monarch's archers guarded the retreat,
Cautioned to stand all deaf to Alca's cries.
Tammac, made beautiful by his desire,
Thanking the gods and blessing justice there,
Reveled with Alca's body, and made sweet

The hour allotted to him, though she spurned
In vain his hot caresses, and was still
Obedient to the law, and nothing more.
And then Bel-shar-uzzur appeared and spake
To Ellac, Chief of Archers, who went forth
And led the panting Alca to the king ;
And as he frowned and bade her no more weep,
Now that the gods were satisfied, a shriek
Was heard within the soiléd bower, and lo !
An archer drew the curtain folds aside
And, with a shout exultant to the king,
Threw Tammac's severed head at Alca's feet,
Such being the will of King Bel-shar-uzzur.
And Alca, free to be his kingly prey,
Was borne in triumph to his perfumed couch,
And blushed not when he crushed her to his arms,
For all her soul went forth in love for him.

Now Ammarac had heard from laughing crowds
The story of the trustless one he loved,
And knew that at that very hour she lay
Throbbing upon the bosom of the king,
And sudden rage stormed at his open heart,
For he desired her with a soldier's love,

A love that had been purely held for her,
A love untainted by a harlot's touch.
And in his grief he knew not what to do.
For many days he dwelt in unconcern,
Haunted by visions of the king's delight,
Haunted by the white roundness of her limbs,
And, reckless, he arose one starry night
To hurl himself upon his rusting lance,
And, for this end, he sought the shrine of Bel,
Begging forgiveness for his coming sin,
And then far from the city's ways he went
To choose a death-spot in the outer ditch,
While, far above, upon the walls, he heard
His soldier-comrades singing in the night:

CHORUS OF SOLDIERS.

Forth from our strongholds we come with a rush and a turbu-
　　lence wonderful,
Smiting the foe unto death, the foe ever boasting and blun-
　　derful,
Ay! like a storm sweeping down, impetuous, terrific and thun-
　　derful!

See! the foe fly in their fear when we charge with heroic
　　audacity!
See them bewildered and crushed by our valor and mad per-
　　tinacity!
How can they stand against us, gaunt lions and bears of
　　rapacity?

Well may they pray to the gods to soften our changeless
　　severity!
Well may they weep and bemoan their preposterous and
　　wretched temerity!
Well may they pray to the gods to defend them from Nebo's
　　asperity!

Well may they tremble and fly, the jest and the jeer of
    humanity !
Well may they curse in the dark on their monarch's ignoble
    insanity !
Under our glittering spears he will writhe in his feminine
    vanity.

Then Ammarac plucked his sick courage up,
And placed the deadly javelin to his heart,
And would have died thinking of Alca's arms
Entwined around the body of his king,
Had not a hand, stretched forward from the dark,
Stayed his first strain, and lo ! before him stood
A bearded savior, a mysterious man,
Grave and majestic, whom he oft had seen,
A wrinkled Jew, a man of holy looks,
Known in the town as Daniel, and a seer.
And Daniel spoke and said : " My worthy son,
Take not the gift of life God gave to thee,
But live, and suffer if thou must, but live !
For it is sin to take thy life, indeed.
I know thy grief, the outrage and the wiles
Of sinful priests, who stripped thee of thy right.
I know the woman thou didst idly woo,

Yea, knew her when a tender girl, and saw
Within her childish eyes the glance of sin,
And prophesied that she would be a toy
For half the town, and it shall come to pass ;
For, weary of the king, Bel-shar-uzzur,
She will depart ere long with many gifts,
And keep a dwelling for the wealthy youth,
And live and die in perfumes and in lust.
Youth ! I have spoken to thee ; mark my words,
And, if thy wounds are far from being healed,
Come unto my abode of purest peace,
Come to the quarter of the hated Jews,
Whose hour of triumph cometh, and relate
Once more with many words thy grievances !"
Then through dark ways the Prophet Daniel led
The stricken warrior toward the Jewish huts,
To listen to his story till the dawn,
And at its end he cried :   " Maltreated friend,
To-morrow I will go unto the king !"

Then from the gloom and horror of the spot
Arose the bitter moan of Hebrew slaves :

"Oh Jehovah !
Hear our prayers.
From the snares
That surround us
And dumfound us,
Where we hover,
Under and over,
Through the city,
Give thy pity !
Deign to guard us,
And discard us
From thee never,
But forever
Give salvation
To thy nation !

" From the awful,
Foul, unlawful
God Bel, painted.
Oh, great sainted,
Proud Jehovah !
Shield and bless us,
Nor distress us !

Isolated,
Beaten, hated,
Generated
Here in error,
We in terror
Pass our lives !
We are goaded
Like beasts loaded,
And our wives,
Sons and daughters
By the waters
Of the city
Work and labor
For their neighbor,
Without pity !
Isolated,
Beaten, hated,
In our sorrow
We can borrow
Consolation
From no human,
Man or woman,
Of this nation !
Men ill treat us,
Scorn and beat us !

Babylon's graves
Are o'ercrowded !
We are shrouded
In the waves
Of the river !
Oh ! deliver
Now thy sons !
Guard thy naked
And unslakéd
Wretched ones
From the rigid
Force and frigid
Clutch of Bel,
Fiend from hell !
Deign to guard us !
Oh ! discard us
From thee never,
But forever
Bring salvation
To thy nation ! "

PART III.

The Medes and Persians thundered at the gates
Impregnable and flawless as the clouds.
And Babylon defied them, for the town
Was sacred as her temples and her gods.
And Cyrus, the invader, knew this thing,
But still would linger prancing near the walls,
Watching his soldiers die by snakes and pest,
While Babylon grew merry, knowing it.

Bel·shar-uzzur, the monarch, in his halls
Of plated pillars and enameled brick,
Gave a great feast unto a thousand lords,
And sat, a god of glory, on his throne
Of carvéd wood draped in embroidered cloth,
Tasseled, and fringed, and glittering with gold.
He held two arrows in his perfumed hand,
For he was king, and eunuchs by his side
Fanned him and held the scented napkins near,
While Alca nestled at his jeweled feet,
And her great eyes were beautiful with flame.

The king was warm with wine, and he arose,
Praising the gods of silver and of gold,

Ay ! and his gods of brass, and wood, and stone,
And cried : "Is this not Babylon the great,
The glory of the East, the queen of towns ? "
And purpled by soft wines he proudly sang :

  "I have my thousands slain !
  The sun on my domain
    Sets never !
  My glory and my fame,
  The terror of my name,
  Consuming like a flame,
    Will last forever !

  " For multitudes of days
  I listen to the praise
    Incessant
  That rises from my land
  To the Egyptian sand ;
  The terror of my hand
    Is ever present !

  " To keep me gemmed and oiled,
  My myriads have toiled
    And striven,

And my victorious star,
As pure as pure Ishtàr,
All enemies afar
    Has driven !

" This holy night we use
The vessels by the Jews
    Once cherished !
The king, now dead, my sire,
Seized them for his desire ;
Jerusalem in fire
    And famine perished !

" Before me it is death
To speak above a breath.
    My glory
Is as god Adar's vast !
And when my hours have passed,
Immortal it will last
    On bricks, in story !

" My beauty is Ishtàr's ;
In me the seven stars
    Are blended,

And in my perfect face
Divinity I trace.
From mighty Nimrod's race
I am descended !

" From Resen and Ashur,
From Opis and Nipur,
　　　My praises,
Over vast mountains blown,
Assault my august throne ;
The fear I cause alone
　　　The world amazes !

" My troops allegiance swear
With the o'erwhelming blare
　　　Of trumpets,
While I, in bliss complete,
Sing, with my perfumed feet
Upon the bellies sweet
　　　Of rosy strumpets !

" I bid a thousand slaves
To dig their own foul graves
　　　Assemble.

All nations hail my worth,
And at my nod all earth
Since my celestial birth
    Doth deer-like tremble !

" I have my thousands slain !
The sun on my domain
    Sets never !
My glory and my fame,
The terror of my name,
Consuming like a flame,
    Will last forever ! "

And lo ! the monarch turned unto his guests
And bade his household laugh, and thereby brake
The grave tradition, which forbade a man
To laugh within the presence of the king.

Therefore the dignitaries of the realm,
Assembled in the cedar banquet hall,
Arose and sang to his delighted ear :

CHORUS.

Of all terrestrial things,
Of all thrice-holy kings,
　　Thou art the fairest !
Of all men seen on earth,
Since sun and stars had birth,
　　Thou art the rarest !

Among the many lords
Who rule the land with swords,
　　Alone thou standest !
For, of all blood and bone
That ever graced a throne,
　　Thou art the grandest !

The damp earth, dark and cold,
Doth rigidly enfold
　　All that thou hatest !
And even the gods on high
In jealous anger cry,
　　Thou art the greatest !

King with the stainless brow !
We to acclaim thee now
     Will be the loudest,
For of all human kind
The gods on earth can find,
     Thou art the proudest !

And then the astrologers of the mighty town,
The grave Chaldeans, wizards among men,
Full of all cunning and for ages wise,
Mathematicians and philosophers,
Conversant with the mysteries of herbs,
Great sorcerers, translators of the stars,
Approached the peerless king and sang to him :

CHORUS OF ASTROLOGERS.

Our great wisdom time defies,
For we read the starry skies
    Like a scroll,
And we know the secrets vast
Of the future, of the past,
    And the soul !

King Bel-shar-uzzur consults
Our wide knowledge, and exults
    When we read,
For we prophesied his reign
Would know famine not, nor pain,
    And no need.

We are old and very wise ;
There is water in our eyes
    When we work ;
But the gods, whom all adore,
When we yield our precious store,
    In us lurk.

We are not like bearded priests,
Who are warm with lust like beasts ;
   We are pure !
In the temple's vaults we dwell,
Of the love of mighty Bel
   We are sure.

We have cut on deathless stone
All the wonders we have known
   In our lives,
And have praised our peerless king
When he deigns to drink and sing
   With his wives !

Bearded Persians dot the plain,
But they strive and strive in vain
   For our fall ;
Their vile bodies Nergal saves
To make green and fat our graves
   When we call !

For we read the starry skies,
Without blunder or surprise,
   Like a scroll,

And we know the secrets vast
Of the future, of the past,
And the soul !

Then suddenly, from nothing, came a HAND
And wrote strange words of fire upon the wall !

"The joints of the king's loins were loosed with fright,"
And tottering on his throne he cried aloud :
" Hark ! whosoever shall this writing read,
And show the interpretation unto me,
He shall be clothed with scarlet, and a chain
Of gold shall be upon his neck, and he
Shall be third ruler of this chosen realm ! "

And as he spake, the palsied courtiers cried
In moaning tones that reached the very stars :

"Strike for us, Bin! in thy majesty invulnerable !
Slay the proud god who in lines of flame sends challenge to
          thee !
Breathe on the words and obliterate them wonderfully !
Crush into naught the insulting, unknown spoliator !
See ! our sweet king faints in terror and is stricken by the
Sight ! Oh, ye gods ! will ye leave him thus to perish in the

Pangs of despair, when your voices, blended gloriously,
Now can avert this calamity and guard us from it?
Oh, perfect El! in thy matchless mercy gaze upon us!
Call in thy wrath for thine angel-host, and mercilessly
Smite with thy dart this assaulting god that terrifies us!
Hurl to the sea, where he spawned in gloom, his insolences!
Oh, god of light! come in storms and fire majestically!
Pass, with fierce winds all the fiery lines obliterating!"

And Daniel came and stood before the king
To read the words of fire, and thus he spake:

"Now that thy grave astrologers make blunder,
Thou callst me, king, to interpret here this wonder,
These lines of fire that came with storm and thunder.

"It is the writing of the Lord Eternal,
Jehovah! whom I praise in prayer diurnal,
The Master of thy impious gods infernal!

"It is a great, imperishable warning,
It is the punishment for all thy scorning,
It is, that thou shalt die before the morning!

" Thy cheeks grow white, Bel-shar-uzzur ! I tell thee
That my high God, ere dawn breaks, will compel thee
To humbly bow before Him and then fell thee !

" Thy wingéd deities lie maimed and wingless ;
Thy soldiers' arrows hurled at God are stingless ;
This haughty town to-morrow will be kingless !

" Thy god of light, thy circle god, thy Shamas,
With all the hosts Assyrian, can not tame us ;
We Jews belong to God !   *Thou* canst not claim us !

" Call on thy Vul, thy Abitur in panic !
Invoke Kalassan's secrets talismanic !
They can not now avert God's wrath volcanic !

" Death comes upon thee, obstinate, rapacious !
Thine empire falls by rites and deeds salacious ;
The vaults of hell await thee, dark and spacious !

" Weighed in the balance, thou art wanting greatly ;
Thy crimes atrocious have grown fouler lately ;
Yea ! in this very palace grand and stately

" Of Israel's daughters thou hast caged the fairest ;
Thy couch revolting with stained souls thou sharest ;
Upon thy brow the scorn of men thou bearest !

" Bel-shar-uzzur ! See in that fire a token :
To-morrow thy proud empire shall be broken !
Bel-shar-uzzur, oh monarch ! I have spoken ! "

And as the dreadful tidings found swift way
Through all the marveling town, the affrighted priests
Rushed to their altars, calling to the gods :

CHORUS.

Before thy blooming brow, oh, God of Terror!
We are but stinking animals in error,
Yea! dung with life, ridiculous and frightful!

Thou must revile us when we bow before thee,
For we are most audacious to adore thee,
For thou art perfect, beautiful, delightful!

Yea! we are toads that hop about thy altar,
But in our slimy heart there never falter
The deathless sources of our adoration.

Our limbs, our lives, our souls are thine forever,
Our lips to worship other gods move never;
For thee we bend our beards in deep prostration!

For thee we seize the rosy, trembling maiden
And lay her panting body, jewel laden,
Upon the silken couch, and hum above her

The Phallic songs to fill her with elation,
And from the highest priests of highest station
We choose for her a tall and perfumed lover.

Ay, while the sacred rites proceed, we fan her
Abundant breast in the all-holy manner,
And watch her beauty blushing into scarlet.

While to attend her in her duty rarest,
Nude women, of the city's women fairest,
Moan in her ears the moanings of the harlot.

Sammuramit the Queen, the great departed,
Pallid with love, hath through this temple darted,
Slave of the Holy Law to once surrender

Her lustrous body to the priest's caresses,
With haunches oiled, with roses in her tresses,
By Beltis made a love-thing warm and tender.

Yea, and the king, Bel-shar-uzzur, the splendid,
Hath entered here when the long day had ended,
To seek untainted flesh for his enjoyment ;

(18)

And we have seen him wreathed with many a couple
Of dancing maidens, flushed with wine, and supple,
Filling his regal veins with gentle cloyment.

Oh, mighty Vul ! the Medes assail our city,
And much alarm us ! On thy slaves have pity ;
Blow them away with devastating thunder,

And to thine altars we will bring a maiden,
Nude as a star, with sweetest lilies laden,
With rosy limbs, a miracle, a wonder !

Far on the plain, among the Medean tents,
Stands Ammarac, a traitor to his king,
Sheltered by Cyrus ; for the foe has sworn
If that an entrance to the town be gained,
Alca, the concubine, shall find release,
And that the king shall perish by swift swords,
Yea, that the king Bel-shar-uzzur shall die,
And after fray and tumult, Ammarac
Shall hold the woman as his slave and toy.
And Ammarac bade all the bearded Medes
To drain the river, turn aside the stream

And fall upon the unsuspecting town.
And this was done, ay ! it so came to pass
That shielded thousands of the people's foes
Filled the great city's heart, before the guards,
Surprised with harlots and warm, sweetened wine,
Were conscious of alarm, and they were slain
By hundreds in the lanes and lighted courts.

Shrill trumpets blared and sounds of war arose,
And shrieks fled echoing to the towers of Bel,
And twenty legions of the Persians, led
By Ammarac in bloody armor, rushed
Unto the banquet hall, where Alca stood
With warm arms round her king, Bel-shar-uzzur,
Who strove to rise, his scepter in his hand ;
But he was hampered by his gold and silk,
And, calling to his gods, the monarch died
With Ammarac's keen javelin in his heart.

Then, while the foe made carrion of the lords,
The warning words of flame upon the wall
Grew dim, and, when the last was swiftly slain,
It disappeared, and the Lord's will was done.

Then Alca, spotted by her lover's blood,
Arose and, standing by the prostrate king,
Cried unto Ammarac : " Approach me not !
Thou hast betrayed thy country and thy king,
And thou to me art fouler than a Jew !
My love, my passion, yea, my soul itself,
Were centered in my monarch thou hast slain ;
And never, by the holy brow of Bel !
Shalt thou know kiss of mine ; and this I swear !
Thy treachery has gained thee no fond prize,
For all my marrows loathe thy crimson hands
And their detested work ! Go forth and slay
The city's babes, thou traitor ! Thou art made
For such a task ! Go ! and be cursed by me !
The day shall never dawn upon my shame ! "
And as she spoke she snatched the dead king's lance,
And fell upon it as a warrior would,
While the red blood choked up her rosy mouth,
While the sweet eyes grew still, and she was dead.

And Ammarac beheld this without tears,
For his poor mind had wandered from its seat,
And forth unto the palace roof he groped,
And leapt into the darkness far below,
Staining an obelisk with guilty blood !

And Babylon was leveled to the dust,
And became heaps as the great prophet said ;
Such was the will of the Almighty God.

CHORUS OF JEWS.

Hail to Jehovah, Jehovah the highest !
Hope of thy people thou never deniest !
   On us and ours hath the Lord taken pity.
Therefore, oh Mighty One ! thankful before thee,
We with humility kneel to adore thee,
   Here in the smoke and the flame of the city !

Now is the power of great Babylon broken !
True were the words that the prophets have spoken !
   Dead are our masters, the lords sacrilegious,
Flown is their might and departed their glory ;
Naught will remain of their impious story ;
   Prone are their gods and their altars prodigious !

Shackled and gyved after slaughter and pillage,
All that are spared of the town will do tillage,
   Ay, in the fields of the conquering nation !
God hath deserted their dwellings forever ;
God will place trust in their promises never ;
   God will not grant them a life of salvation !

Great is thy wrath, oh Jehovah! and lawful,
Just are thy punishments, rapid and awful!
  Righteous, deserved is this nation's affliction,
For thou hast promised to guide us and love us,
Now and forever in glory above us,
  Sacred and pure by thy sweet benediction!

May 15, 1882.

LOT'S WIFE.

LOT'S WIFE.

Sodom in all the splendor of her towers,
The monumental miracle and grace
Of all the haughty cities of the plain,
Throbbed and exulted in her love of life,
Like some great marble monster animate.
Beyond the bristling circuit of the walls,
Peopled by glittering sentinels at arms,
Stretched in a flowerful labyrinth of green
The leafy loveliness of Siddim's vale,
Teeming with orchards of ancestral trees,
Alive with grazing flocks and myriad birds,
A revel and delight of clustering vines,
Dotted with tranquil lakes and bastioned hills
Unto the limits of the Arkite lands.

Blessed by the Lord, the ever fecund soil
Was prosperous with surfeit of gold grain,
Yielding a ready increase through the years

To feed the grand and colossean town,
Which shone above it in its lordliness
Like some immense, bewildering star of steel.

Within the triple armor of her walls,
Sodom, impregnable, awaited night,
Arrayed in the sharp dazzle of her lamps,
In countless thousands lighting the large ways ;
Waited, while sultry summer's twilight came
To cool its heart of marble with kind dews,
And breathe the perfume of awakening flowers.

Circled by budding leagues of fair parterres,
A hundred holy temples thrust their domes
And miracles of many-pillared grace
High to the stars in grandeur insolent,
Where bizarre figures, fashioned into gods,
Guarded the dizzy steps and jasper stairs
Leading to pyramids and tapering towers,
While on the ample palace roofs, in charm
And luxury prodigious, breathed and bloomed
A world of swaying gardens beautiful.

Here on the avenues, where roses seemed
To grow more plentiful than a forest's weeds,
Stood in a maze of porphyry and gold
The peerless statues of the inviolate gods,
And wondrous idols crushed with lucent gems,
In pillared temples vast, miraculous.
Here brooded Nergal in his awful calm,
Upon his puissant altars, in his hand
The scintillant sword that nations terrified.
Alone, supreme, majestic, he looked down
Upon the attendant throngs of bearded priests,
Stern in the splendors of his scarlet robes,
While in his outstretched hand a human head
Dropped in dull splashes its fast clotting gore,
Staining the lapis steps with ruddy red.

Around him, in the close prophetic gloom,
Were awful shapes of animals and men,
Bewildering images of unknown forms,
Accouplements of monsters and of birds
With shapely maidens and exulting slaves,
Figures of great divinities and powers
Deigning to germinate with earthly flesh,
And sensual minglements of flowers and brutes,

Where loves amorphous charmed the radiant gods,
And where audacious lust stood glorified.

Here rose the reeking altar-grees of Bel,
And Yem, the king of the exalted gods,
And Bar, the hero of all heroes, stood
In lustrous bronze beside all potent Nin,
With Bita, king of oceans and of fish,
And Anu, holier than the holy stars.

Here reigned the great and terror-dealing Beltis,
The pure, impeccable and beauteous goddess,
And in the perfumed temple's gloom before her
Maidens would swoon in holy prostitution,
Adoring her fecundity and beauty,
Filling the temple with their sighs of rapture,
Low and delicious like the doves' soft cooing.
Here would they wait to lure the idle passer,
Tempting his glance by bare and fragrant bosoms,
Calling upon their goddess and Sheruba,
Divine Ishtàr, and lily-limbed Anuta,
To make their flesh a love-light and a wonder,
To win the timorous stranger and the passer.
Their languid limbs were radiant with jewels ;

Their thighs were smeared with warm, voluptuous
    ointments,
And tiars of gold coin amid their tresses
Shone in the gloom like the fond eyes of angels.
They smiled and languished in their lustful dreaming,
Watching their eyes flash in their copper mirrors,
Beautiful, redolent, supple-limbed and tempting,
Carelessly tapping on their noisy tabrets,
Screened by the goddess in the temple's arches,
Yearning for some sweet stripling of the city,
Or the grave, palm-oiled warriors of Gomorrah,
And, as they toyed with gold and silver ouches,
Prayed unto Hea to relieve and send them
Some dainty zonah, some delicious zonah,
Who, lacking lovers, would with joy caress them,
Ay, love them sweetlier for lacking lovers.

Within Ashurs' colossal almug temple,
Around the holy altar sacrificial,
Drowsy with cassia fumes and stringent spices,
The heady nekoth, the sweet smell of heaven,
Lying and dozing with the sacred serpents,
Listening to eunuchs idly thrum the viol,
Nodding their chins upon their tuneless nebels.

Linger the chosen lovers of the altar,
Perfumed and supple, in a gaudy raiment,
Oiled to the beard and like fresh lilies fragrant,
Drenched with basam, and cinnamon's sweet juices,
Praying to Anu to secure them lovers;
Lovers who would reward their warm caresses
With costly gifts of onycha and ointment;
Lovers who lavish galbanum in plenty,
When cloyed and satisfied with their embracing,
And they to all will amorously pander,
Being of loves mysterious and strange passions
The slaves, the chosen and the perfect masters.

There in the inner gloom, like a strong wind,
Arose the high priest's grave, majestic song:

SONG OF PRIESTS.

Oh, sacred Nergal! on thy high throne stately,
Protect us now, for we respect thee greatly.
  Judge of the golden scepter, vast and holy,
Guard us from evil's messengers, we pray thee.
Our lives are given and fettered to obey thee.
  We worship thee alone, thy glory solely!

Thou art alone our master pure and rightful;
In thee are all things perfect and delightful;
  Thou, thou alone of heavenly kings art regal!
We bow before thee in our utter rankness,
In all our sin's ignoble, naked frankness;
  Thy mandates to our souls are ever legal.

For thee, oh Nebo, thunderful and glorious!
We, thy poor slaves, are loving and laborious;
  Around thy shrines the zonahs strike loud cymbals.
Dawn, day and night we worship and we praise thee
With holy brass, and golden altars raise thee,
  Amid the clashing of a thousand tymbals.
  (19)

Before thy brow multipotent and lustrous,
Bow countless legions of the rabble blustrous,
 Before thy holy sword that flashes lightning,
Ay, to thy throne of spices and of scarlet,
The priest, the slave, the stranger and the harlot
 Come on their knees thy praises ever heightening.

Each day thy templed grees are stained and gory
With human blood to sanctify thy glory ;
 Our crimson hands for thee are never idle,
For thee we slay the tamar-scented maiden
Who with strong faith approaches, jewel-laden,
 To woo thee by her death to awful bridal.

To thee our king, great Bera proud and splendid,
Prays on his knees when the cool dawn hath ended,
 He, of all earthly kings the puissant leader,
Who brings thee tribute of sweet nard delicious,
Stacte and gold to crave thy glance propitious,
 With many slaves, and cinnamon and cedar !

Before thy throne majestic, god tremendous !
Crawl in a drowsy ecstasy, stupendous,
 The sacred serpents in calm adoration ;

They curl around thy worshipers who perish,
Crushed in damp folds, but, dying, only cherish
　　The hope to win thy smile as compensation.

Oh Nergal! in thy many-pillared palace,
Be not unto our supplications callous ;
　　See us with blood upon our brows, and bless us,
Give us thy strength to battle with the foemen,
Open our souls by thy portentous omen,
　　And spare us, master, for our sins distress us !

The night had come ; the city was aflame
With lust, and music, and continual song,
And through the crowded streets the people passed,
Unconscious of the dawning of a care.
Shinab, the King of Admah, with a suite
Of many chieftains of his tribe, had come
To bow before King Bera, Sodom's king,
And King Shemeber, lord of Zeboim,
And Birsha, the divine and holy one,
King of Gomorrah, the great sister town,
Having saluted all the city's gods,
And having filled the city's ways with gold,

Were seated in King Bera's banquet hall
And entertained by melodies of harps.
And all the people praised the god-given kings,
Chatted, and were most merry of their lives,
And mocked the moon, and laughed with strangers
　　there.

Then the gay zonah, bearing her silk tent,
Passed by and flashed her lovely eyes about,
To tempt the people to come in with her,
And in her luring beauty paused and sang :

SONG.

Oh, sweet passer ! I am fair,

For the lily scents my hair,

Made most redolent and glossy by the radiant roses' oil ;

My ringed arms are dazzling white,

And my kiss is a delight,

While the sweet alhenna clusters burn my bosom while I toil.

Like my goddess, great Ishtàr,

My black glance outshines a star,

And my form is warm and wavy, like the palm and the tamar ;

I have sapphires and rare gems

On my mantle's scarlet hems,

And the unguents on my haunches come o'er deserts from afar.

I hold, hidden in my tent,

Drugs of love and ravishment,

And a bed where fragrant lilies lie with birdlings' downy
plumes ;

    I hold passion and desire
    To inspire love's sleepy fire,
And to stir the sullen pulses in soft aromatic glooms !

    Till the midnight I will sing
    Unto Nebo, the great king,
And my asor's gentle music will allay thy fevered rest ;
    Thou shalt slumber till my birds
    Wake to hear my loving words,
While I press a thrice-born passion on the marble of my breast.

    The pure night is waning fast ;
    Oh, my god Yem, unsurpassed !
Send me golden lovers many, ay, if only for a span !
    And, oh passers wise and brave !
    Be not tempted by yon slave,
For my kisses are far sweeter than the kisses of a man !

Then from the surging multitude one man,
A Hamathite, so reckoned by his beard,
Curly and redolent with sickening spice,
Spake to the attentive zonah and took gold,

Three golden pieces from his inner belt,
And went with her, while all the people laughed,
For he, a stranger, knew not that her kiss
Was purchasable for a silver bit.

And while they laughed an old man sauntered by,
Reeking with drugs and spices to the nails,
His ears were ringed with monstrous Hivite coins ;
Great golden bracelets clasped his nervous arms ;
His sandals were besprent with many pearls,
And his loose robes were woven of rustling things.
The people ceased all laughter, as a bird
Ceases to sing when arrows hurt the air,
And he, the white-haired, paused, and with a voice
Shrill as the sound of flinty rocks when rubbed,
Smiled through his colors and sang, even thus:

SONG.

Come to me, all ye who burn
For a passion in return !
There are perfumes on my body and fresh leaves upon my
    hair ;
I am sleek and very wise,
I know woman's softest sighs,
And my kisses warm and manly all the senses can ensnare.

I am old, ay, very old,
And my price is bricks of gold,
Being chief and holy master of the lovers of the town.
I am high priest unto Bel,
In the grace of Vul I dwell,
And the motion of my pleasure is a song and a renown !

I have been the pampered slave
Of King Amraphel, the grave,
I have swooned and slumbered often in King Chedorlaomer's
    arms.

There is gold within my house,
There are jewels on my brows,
And my breast is warm and tender as an Arkite maiden's
    charms !

I have drugs to warm afresh
The dull failings of the flesh,
I have grateful food and spices, and suave basams honey-pure,
And when laggard from excess
Of my amorous caress,
I will sing thee Nergal's praises on the many-stringed kinoor.

See ! the dawn is coming soon ;
There is slumber in the moon ;
Hasten, passer ! hasten, stranger ! to my tent's enticing shade.
Be not tempted by the cry
Of the zonahs strutting by,
For my kisses are far sweeter than the kisses of a maid !

Then came a youth who paused amid the crowd,
Browed like a king and lovely as the stars.
His beard was merry with exotic spice,
And there was love within his perfect eyes ;
He was well sandaled, and he sang this wise :

SONG.

Oh, sweet passer! I am strong,
Grace and charm to me belong ;
All my flesh is like soft sammet and my muscles rival steel ;
I have spices on my breast ;
My dark locks are oiled and tressed,
And the wounds of suffering passion I can mollify and heal.

Hark, all ye who round me throng,
I can sing a lulling song,
I can charm you with the cadence of my rich sonorous voice,
And with suave, melodious words,
Sweeter far than trills of birds,
I can win your languid pleasure and can make the soul rejoice !

To our king one festal night
I gave rapture and delight,
And he crowned my brows with myrtle, ay ! and kissed me on
his throne ;

For my beauty is as rare

As Askar's, surnamed the Fair,

And the secrets of sweet passion unto me belong alone !

There is ever new surprise

In the poem of mine eyes ;

I am lithe, and light, and supple, like the leopard of the plain ;

My curled hair has reached the length

Of the lion's in his strength,

And my kiss is warm and fragrant like the falling of the rain !

I have zonahs in my house,

With white lilies on their brows,

To excite you by soft kisses and white perfume-reeking arms,

While I beckon your embrace

In the splendor of my grace,

While you play in joy ecstatic with the beauty of their charms !

Oh, sweet passer ! do not heed

Yon old creature in his need,

For his words are false and worthless, and a century,dims his
    fire ;

He gives herbs and venomed roots ;

His cold kiss is like a brute's,

And the spasms of god-like passion his decrepit carcass tire !

Come to me, all ye who crave
The sweet passion of a slave !
Bring me gold, or wine and honey, and my kisses will be yours ;
And I swear by mighty Bel
To anoint and please you well,
While my naked zonahs press you, and the balmy night
endures !

And ere the last dull sound had left his lips,
Men crowded near him with uncurbed desire,
Feeling his feeble limbs and bargaining there
To learn his secrets and the joys thereof ;
And with a citizen, who spake of gold
In unclipped bricks, and silver coin beside,
He left the streets, and no one stirred or smiled ;
While envy for a moment dusked all brows,
For some had coin, but owned no golden bricks.

King Bera, with his beard curled like a rose,
Lay on his cushions near the regal board,
Laden with savory meats and bursting fruit,
Honey, and heating herbs, and sweetened wines ;
While near his sceptered hand lay Birsha, king
Of high Gomorrah, sacred as the gods,

And on inferior mats of violet wool,
Burning with fear and envy to their eyes,
Sat Shinab, king of Admah, and the lord
And sacred king Shemeber, who had come
From Zeboim with high tributes to the gods,
To Bel, the procreator, they had prayed,
To Vul, the god of atmospheres ; and, lo !
They were an hungered and were worn of prayer,
And listened to the melodies of lutes,
That pleased and soothed them as they humbly ate.

Then did Ashcar, the favorite of the king,
His laughing counselor and his body's friend,
One whom he loved with all surpassing love,
And who from birth was destined for his bed,
Being of princely blood in his own right,
Arise, and, merry with the warming wine,
Sing to the god-king, thrumming the asor :

SONG OF THE KING'S FAVORITE.

Mighty Bera, no one raises
Unto thee the praise of praises ;
Every day thy people hail thee
With the songs that are the same.
With no blame dare they assail thee,
Or with merry meaning flail thee,
And the gods in wrath forsake them in their unprolific shame !

I will sing thy praises splendid,
Which on earth have never ended ;
I will tell the tribes in wonder
Of thy prowesses unknown ;
I will prove, and without blunder,
That above the stars or under
There are none who boast the glories that to thee belong alone !

Are there in thy cities many
Happy, valiant soldiers, any
Who can smoothe the perfumed tresses
Of a lithe and brawny slave,

And with rapturous caresses
Wear his spirit by excesses,
As thou canst, oh, wondrous master ! when strong passions in
    thee rave ?

Are there any monarchs near thee,
Who implore thee and who fear thee,
Who can tire in soft prostration
The dark maidens of the town,
With such fleshly adulation,
With such virile animation,
As thine own, oh, haughty monarch ! of all terror and renown ?

No ! thou art alone, oh master !
And my praises, swelling faster,
Must as god of gods acclaim thee
In the splendor of thy loins ;
For no draining love can tame thee,
Nor can lover's deeds ashame thee,
When a fever with sweet passion in thy robust bosom joins !

Thou art God, supreme and holy,
To be loved and worshiped solely,
For thy breast is filled with gladness
And thine eyes all foes destroy !

In thy flesh there is no badness,
No corruption, and no sadness,
And the offal of thy body is a perfume and a joy !

Loud swelled the laughter, and the cymbals clashed ;
The puissant king made sign, and to them came
Nude girls with starry eyes and scented hair,
Dancing in dreamy posturings, that made
The wine-warm bosoms of the kings expand,
And cry aloud : "Bel ! thou alone art great !"
Their eyes grew lustrous, for the Sodom drugs
Had breathed hot poison in their slavish veins,
And, to the sound of titillating lutes,
King Shinab rose in ecstasy's first throe,
Clasping a maiden in his close embrace ;
And haughty Birsha, great Gomorrah's king,
Chose for his own an Ardavitish slave,
Whose limbs were like great serpents coiled in flesh ;
And in a wanton slumber Sodom's king
Lay, languid, in the smiling Ashcar's arms,
While high in utter heaven the tranquil stars
Shed streams of silver on the illumined town,
Crowning with light the insolent debauch,

And, as the mighty monarchs swooned and writhed
In joys ineffable, from the open courts
Arose the voices, on the bastions near,
Of bearded soldiers singing to the moon :

CHORUS OF THE WARRIORS OF SODOM.

By sweet love we are not weak,
And our vengeance we can wreak
Upon any foe audacious who doth dare to stand before us !
There is danger in our eyes,
There is slaughter in our cries,
When the blaring trumpets thunder and our banners flutter
o'er us.

We have fallen like a rain
On the cowards of the plain.
We have thrust our glittering lances in their bosoms un-
victorious.
We have faced the Girgashites
And the haughty Jebusites,
And have made the valley pregnant with their carcasses
inglorious !

The Rephaim we have sought
In their fastnesses, and fought
With these monsters than trees taller, all in iron and armor
shielded.

We have met them face to face,
And by Vul's immortal grace
We have stricken and have felled them till their haughty
spirit yielded!

Amraphel of far Shinar,
In his burnished battle-car,
We have met upon the meadows in the combat fierce and
frantic,
And have saved from heroes' graves
Even his sons, to be our slaves,
And have crushed his power triumphant by our prowesses
gigantic!

Oh, sweet Anu, if our king,
Holy Bera, with the sting
Of our lashing swords and lances will allow us to adore thee,
On the Hittites we will fall,
And their chiefs and maidens all
We will smite, and slay, and ravish, and in thousands bring
before thee!

For we weary of all rest;
There is rust upon our breast,
And we tire of Sodom's splendor and the pretty zonah's tattle!

There are foemen in the plain ;
Lead us onward there again,
Oh, great Nergal ! while we languish for the glories of the
    battle !

And echoing the defiance of their throats,
In Vul's dark sanctuary the high priests sang :

"Oh, mighty Nergal ! guard our sacred city ;
Watch us and bless us in thy holy pity ;
    Lighten our brows and waft thy blessings o'er us ;
Give us the strength all time to bow before thee ;
Give us eternal seasons to adore thee,
    And we will praise thee through our brass sonorous !"

Then the sweet wings of night upon the town
Were softly spread, and all its ways were still.

PART II.

Now Lot, the son of Haran, dwelt within
    The city's walls and loved its many ways ;
    But he was pure of heart unto his praise,
And much deplored all God-defying sin.

He lived estranged from the licentious throng,
   Doting upon the fairness of his wife,
   Proud of the blameless quiet of his life,
A righteous man and unashamed of song.

For he had sisters twain, alert and gay,
   Milcah and Iscah, and their voices, blent
   In praise to God, would send a ravishment
Unto him, at the twilight of the day.

His cares were many, having many tents,
   Asses and numerous flocks, and camels, too ;
   And he was judge, and had just deeds to do,
Though there was little for his recompense.

His tastes were simple, for he loved his herds,
   His silent oxen with imploring eyes,
   And loved to see them graze, for he was wise,
And smiled at the sweet trebles of his birds.

He praised the beauteous advent of the spring,
   And the rare, fructuous loves of heaven and earth ;
   Their beauteous nuptials brought prolific birth,
Like rain on meadows when the sparrows sing.

And he was fain to worship and adore
   In his heart's secrecy a higher god
   Than Nergal, who to him was but a clod ;
And he was rich enough to scent his floor.

Now Ilcah, Lot's fair wife, in Sodom born,
   Was in her sullied heart adverse to him ;
   Because his eyes by labor had grown dim,
She suffered by his love in silent scorn.

For he was like old dreamers in the night,
   Loving to doze and ponder on his herds,
   And even his infrequent passion words
Were tame unto her, offering no delight.

She, in the blooming May-time of her years,
   With passionate eyes and lustrous veils of hair,
   Yearned for love's ecstasy and its despair,
A love of laughter, ravishment and tears.

And she, grown weary of Lot's grave renown,
   Would seek the city's heart on festal days,
   And strut like zonahs on its marble ways,
For she adored a man within the town,

One whom her girlish spirit idolized,
    A valorous chief, a most athletic man,
    With mighty limbs, known as the lord Suran,
Who for his famed virility was prized.

And he had led her to Vul's temple, where,
    Ravished by his bright armor and the glance
    Of conquering eyes, in a voluptuous trance
She veiled his breast with all her loosened hair.

And while the priests officiating cried :
    " Give to great Vul, oh women ! all your charms ! "
    She lay amort with love within his arms,
And on his perfumed bosom softly sighed.

And he, for she was ravenous to learn,
    Taught her the mysteries and the holy rites
    That steeped her bosom in unknown delights,
Strange pressures, and new minglements that burn !

And she revered the aroma of his beard,
    Giving her radiant body for his play,
    And in the temple in the hot midday,
Alone, to tempt his vigor she appeared.

Veiled to the eyes, but amorous of the spot,
 Loving the sensual magic of the gloom,
 Seeking sweet impious bonds that foster doom,
Her heart made merry by her scorn of Lot.

Her limbs were maddened by strong Suran's touch ;
 She sang to him in passionate unrest ;
 His curléd head was warm upon her breast ;
His flanks were fruitful, and she loved him much.

Ay, with such adoration that, to fill
 His lecherous eyes with raptures held so dear,
 She would have braved cold death without a fear,
If, following, Suran would have loved her still !

To please his whim at the great autumn feast,
 Held to Vul's glory on the dying year,
 Rosy and nude, fair Ilcah did appear,
Surrendering her beauty to the priest.

Ay, in the holy vaults, for Suran's sake,
 She learned the arcana of the zonahs there,
 Slumbering with women amorous and bare,
So that he, too, in pleasure might partake.

And she in beauty through the temple trod,
   Warm with her loves and flushed by flowers and wine,
   Hailing her prostitution as divine
And most delightful, worthy of her god.

And Lot had honored her with manly trust,
   And let the days pass dreaming of his herds,
   Counting his kine and listening to his birds,
Serenely unsuspicious and most just.

Now God was angered at the vice of Sodom.
Each day her sins became more bold and grievous.
Lust was abroad upon her many highways,
And it was worshiped in a throng of temples.
So He resolved to chastise and to doom it
With scorching flame, alert and purifying.

And Abraham, a man of prayer and holy,
A friend to Lot, who loved him like a father,
Implored the Lord in humble intercession,
And stood before Him, desolate and anxious,
Crying: "O Lord! if Thou this town destroyest,
Thou mayest in Thy wrath destroy the guiltless,

Who much abhor the awful dereliction
Of their lost brethren, deaf to prayer or pity.
Spare Thou the town for their sake, oh Jehovah!
If in its tainted tents I can discover
Fifty whose hearts are pure, and peradventure
I may by such a proof appease Thy rancor!"
And God consented; then did Abraham boldly,
For his whole heart was beautiful and noble,
Implore again, braving the Lord's displeasure:
"For ten's sake only, wilt Thou still forgive it?"
Such was his tenderness for unhappy Sodom;
And the Lord listened and again consented
To count the upright souls and save the city.

Veiling their heavenly essence, vaguely hoping,
The angels passed into the town atrocious,
Seeking Lot's home for sympathy and shelter,
For they were beautiful in their disguises,
And roused swift passion in the men that saw them
Pass in grave radiance through the city's portals.
And Lot, bewildered by their coming, startled
By lustful cries of many at his doorway,
Concealed them in the darkness of his chamber,
And offered to the throng his nubile daughters;

Ay, for his hospitality was sacred,
And the vile rabble who had greatly lusted
For the white strangers, and their beauty only,
Hurried on elsewhere in their anger, baffled,
Cursed him aloud and spat upon his threshold.

Then came to Lot the pale, affrighted angels,
Saying : "Good man, thy life is now in danger!
Within these walls accursed can be no pardon.
The people for their infamy must perish ;
Such is the will of the Lord God Jehovah!
And with our eyes we can not see salvation,
Nor have we now the power to avert destruction.
We must return to the Eternal Father,
For He hath spoken, and we know His meaning.
Sodom is doomed to be a smoking desert,
Shorn of its gods, its roses and its temples,
Covered with briars and labyrinths of brambles,
Stricken by scourging salt and burning sulphur,
And on its ruins there will be no planting,
Ay, on its ruins there will be no sowing!
Therefore we warn thee, for thy soul is righteous ;
Arise and call thy family together,
Iscah and Milcah, thy devoted sisters,

And with them and the wife thou lovest, Ilcah ;
Depart from out the city with great caution,
Ay, with thy flocks, ay, even with thy cattle,
And seek another land of grain and plenty.
Fear not, kind Lot, for Abraham will be near thee ! "
And then, saluting Lot with smiling kindness,
They spread their wings and waved their white way
          upward !
And o'er the glare and tattle of the city,
Like a great star of light in woody darkness,
They paused and sang a piteous lamentation :

SONG OF THE ANGELS.

We flew with white wings fluttering o'er the nation,
Bearing God's promise of divine salvation,
If worthy men were found in prayer's prostration.

We sought the righteous, pure of heart and holy,
The priest-deceived, the ignorant, the lowly,
Those who for sinning do not languish solely,

Those who unto the boundless skies aspire,
Who live and hope that fate holds something higher
Than bestial altars stained with blood and fire,

But we have failed, and in our indignation
We have beheld, with cries and lamentation,
Enormous sin, idolatry, stupration,

Ignoble rites of brutishness horrific,
Pollution infamous to the Omnific,
Disgusting lust and revelries morbific!

We fail to find a spirit pure and blameless !
The town is feverish with passions shameless,
Atrocious cries and prostitution nameless,

False worship hideous, sacrifice diurnal
Unto a sceptered clod, a god infernal,
Orgies and crime, defying the Eternal !

We will away ! Our prayers can no sin sunder ;
Corruption sways the town above and under ;
We leave it to God's lightning and His thunder !

Now Ilcah, trifling with her favorite birds,
Had heard in vague dismay the angels' words,
And to the bastion where proud Suran kept
His mighty vigil she with caution crept,
And spake to him in feverish unrest,
Panting and timid, by great fears possessed,
For doubt had dawned within her, and she feared
The unknown God that Abraham revered.
And Suran mocked her and her child-alarms,
For he was fain to hold her in his arms,
And see the perfect summer of love's June
Mantle her cheeks below the mellow moon.

With many jests he won her fears away,
Soothed her worn thoughts and tempered her dismay,
And lied with fervor, saying he had seen,
Crouched in Vul's temple, near the holy screen,
The white-faced strangers, ay, the angels fair,
Enter, and choosing from the zonahs there,
Depart unto the temple's inner shrine.
Heated with lust and radiant with wine,
Ay, even so, he cried: " But, Ilcah, sweet,
If the sad town this threatened doom must meet,
I, warned and ready by thy love for me,
Will be alert, and I will follow thee,
Ay, to another land, beneath new stars,
I swear it by the grace that is Ishtàr's,
I swear it by the lengthy beard of Bel ;
This will I do, for I do love thee well ! "
Then, like a weary bird that finds its nest,
Calm and content, she lingered on his breast.

The pure dawn came, and Lot, with wrinkled brows
Made dull by care and most engrossing thought,
Bade Ilcah and his servant men prepare
And leave the town, adding no other word,
Save that the Lord had bidden him do the same,
For doom impendent hovered on the town,

And that, when far upon the Siddim plain,
No soul should turn to see the city's fate,
Or cast a pitying glance upon its shame ;
Such was the will of God ; and if in fear
An eager eye unto the bastions turned,
Then would the disobedient suffer death !

So they went forth in silence and deep pain,
While night, impenetrable, veiled the plain.
Then the Lord spake, and lo ! the ominous thunder
Was heard about His brows in fury gathering !
Wan sheets of lurid lightning writhed and scattered
The battling clouds united to impede them,
With walls of rain and leagues of seething vapor.
Down through the shields of mist His bolts were driven;
Unleashed and maddened o'er the universes,
In glowing seconds did they swiftly traverse
Spaces illimitable, nameless distance,
Before, in strength tremendous concentrating,
In dizzy worlds of fire they hurried downward.

They fell with wrath vertiginous and awful
Upon the puny jasper of Vul's temple,
Striking to nothingness the giant columns,
Blow upon blow, so swift that they were painless,

Scythed the deep, serried ranks of priests attending,
And lingered in a moving mass horrific
Upon the domes, ere rising to the heavens
Again to fall, leading death's cortège with them.
Hope there was none, and there was nowhere shelter.
Severe, implacable, a flood of brimstone
And searching fire from the wild heaven descended,
While the earth trembled in stupendous travail,
And upon hosts of blanchened victims opened.
Loud o'er the hell of flame arose in anguish
The dolorous shrieks of nations pale and hideous,
Begging their gods in agony to spare them,
While o'er the imploring palms and wrinkled foreheads
The haughty palaces and great domes tottered,
And unto dust the granite bastions crumbled !
Fire, fire, eternal fire their homes assaulted,
And there was madness, but no sweet salvation !

Pale and dismayed, the king, the mighty Bera,
Fled from his throne in silence and in terror,
Fled to the streets where everywhere around him
Lay his crushed hosts of people and supporters,
While o'er the fire a mighty invocation
Rose from the priests, his sanctity surrounding :
 (21)

" Oh, lofty Vul ! from thy marble beauty gaze upon us ;
Spare in thy wrath thine adorers, who are stricken by the
Fire that hath dared on thy temple's glory insolently
Now to fall fast, all thy holy secrets desecrating !
Turn in thy rage on the god afflicting outrage on thee ;
Crush with thy glance all his hidden, haughty emis-
    saries ;
Spread in the soul of the cruel slayer, mercilessly,
Fear of thy hand that alone can banish torment from us !
Strike, awful Vul ! and hurl back to heaven wonder-
    fully
All the fierce flame that is desolating thy eternal
Shrine, and we all will with sacrifices glorify thee,
Ay, as our god, and will worship thee perpetually ! "

And as they cried, the heavens were rent again,
And swifter, fiercer, fell the blighting rain !

    Far to the south, directed by God's grace,
    Lot had made hasty progress from the place
        For many a weary hour,
    Beseeching the high Lord with eyes cast down
    To mitigate the anguish of the town
        And stay His dooming power.

He dared not linger to erect his tents
Or take repose, such was his soul's suspense ;
    Nor did he dare turn back
Where the dull rumble of the starless sky
Warned him the fatal chastisement was nigh,
    And where the heavens grew black !

He heard with consternation in his soul
The gathering masses of the thunder roll ;
    He heard the cities cry ;
He saw the avalanche of fire descend
From shaken space, ay, without any end,
    And knew that all would die !

He saw above, below, and everywhere
A universal and all-blinding glare,
    And bolts that burst and burn.
Of his own given salvation he knew not ;
He only knew he gave the word of Lot,
    And, therefore, did not turn.

Pity with terror battled in his eyes ;
He palmed his ears to escape the city's cries ;
    He wept for the undone.

He found no solace in the calm of prayer ;
He was all torture, trembling and despair,
  But, resolute, went on.

Then Ilcah, while the great metropolis blazed,
Fell shuddering to her knees, disheveled, crazed,
  Trembling with guilty dread,
And to his heart, to all compassion steeled,
In consternation and in tears appealed
  To turn his steps instead.

"Thy God is cruel, arrogant, unjust,
If thus He strikes the innocent to dust,
  Slaying, when life He gave !
Turn, oh my husband ! oh mine honored Lot !
Let us return unto the wretched spot !
  Lift up thy voice to save ! "

And Lot in deep dejection sadly cried :
" The Lord hath willed this in His injured pride ;
  I, slave, must Him obey.
Pause not, nor turn, for here and everywhere
His wrath is visible and will not spare !
  Arise and come away ! "

Then from the spreading havoc of the flame
Rose on the startled air fair Ilcah's name !
    The voice she did adore
Called out in agony : " Oh, Ilcah mine !
Be merciful !   Recall the love once thine ;
    Save me ! I can no more !

" Thy Suran calls thee ; hasten ere too late ;
The fire hath bitten my feet, oh ! do not wait !
    The hot air chokes my cry !
Ilcah ! oh Ilcah ! all my soul doth burn !
Return, oh salvatory love ! return !
    Save me, or else I die ! "

Then like a tigress of her young despoiled,
She looked on Lot, while he in shame recoiled,
    And cried : " Thou wilt not save
Yon helpless man, oh ! coward that thou art,
When impious rains from hated heaven dart
    To make his fiery grave !

" I curse thee, graybeard, and thy God malign !
That voice is Suran's, he is the divine
    Sweet lover of my soul !

He is my hope, my life and my delight,
My god by day, my star of love by night,
　　My ravishment, my goal !

" Thou weeping, loathsome craven ! go thy way,
Cursed by my hate until thy carrion day !
　　Go to thy God revered !
I love him in the ruin and the fire !
He is my Lord Jehovah and desire !
　　Go, for I curse thy beard !

" Death in his loyal arms is far more sweet
Than life with thee in misery complete !
　　With him 'twere good to die !
Go on thy hated way, go ! go ! obey
Thy nauseous God of ruin and decay !
　　I to his arms will fly ! "

And with all Sodom's beauty in her eyes,
Rosy with rage, and passion, and surprise,
　　Towards the great plains that burned,
Fearless of death, irradiant and grand,
In woman's love transfigured she did stand,
　　And in defiance turned !

Swift through the sheets of blinding fire and hail,
Hoping against all mortal hope, and pale,
    Proud in her noble love,
Made by her heart's nobility thrice pure,
She hurried toward him o'er the fearful moor,
    Scoffing the wrath above !

And with her arms around his panting breast,
Her refuge, her salvation and her rest,
    Once more she laid her head,
While in a crown a flame, sublime, irate,
The fires of heaven her love did consecrate
    And fiercer on them sped.

"Suran, oh love ! fear not, our gods are strong !
This dire affliction will not linger long !
    In Vul's sweet heaven release
For our poor, tortured and indignant souls
We there shall find, and, oh ! delicious goals
    Of everlasting peace !

"Suran, I love thee ! Press me closer still !
The desolating flame itself is chill
    To my love's endless flame !

Kiss me again ! Blot out this world of pain !
Ay, so again, sweet Suran, so—again ! "

*   *   *   *   *

And then the lightning came.

SONG OF ANGELS.

See the dire fate of the proud cities blamable,
Blind with foul lust and all passions untamable,
  Made by sad sin to high heaven importunate !
Once were they powerful, and dreaded, and numberless ;
Now are their souls for eternity slumberless,
  Doomed to the flames, oh, rebellion unfortunate !

Fed with the fevers of fearful idolatry,
Steeped to the soul in supreme demonolatry,
  Tainted with crime toward the Angels censorious,
Crushed by the thunder-bolts' pitiless density,
Perished, departed, in awful immensity,
  Dread ye the fate of their ending inglorious !

They in their beauty and arrogant fearlessness
Soiled with debauch Nature's law in its peerlessness,
  Spurning Jehovah in haughty impiety,

Heedless of chastisement, scorning futurity,
Mocking His word and His promise of purity,
  Glad of their vices adored to satiety !

Guided by priests full of cunning and lechery,
Slaves to the monarchs whose promise was treachery,
  How could they love the Creator and, dutiful,
Seek in His bosom of tempered austerity
Pardon and love, and adorable verity,
  Charity hallowed, and faith ever beautiful ?

. No ! They did spurn and reject Him distrustfully,
Pleased with the Mages who conquered them lustfully,
  Pleased by their worship of flesh and immanity,
Till the high heavens, defied by salacity,
Punished with thunder their nameless audacity,
  Crushed them and doomed their rebellious insanity !

So they shall suffer for odious carnality,
Now and forever, to all immortality,
  And the great God they have outraged diurnally,
Hath to the world that rolls wondering under us
Sworn from the height of His Majesty thunderous
  Pardon to none through the ages eternally !

No mercy dwelt in God's avenging hand,
No pity turned His anger from the land,
And, when the day, made laggard by affright,
Dawned on the earth in miracles of light,
The guilty towns, that dared to disobey,
Their temples and their gods had passed away !